CONVENIENT

Fall

PLAYERS OF MARYCLIFF UNIVERSITY
BOOK 2

JERICA MACMILLAN

Convenient Fall
Book 2 Players of Marycliff University
Jerica MacMillan
Copyright © 2016 by Jerica MacMillan

ISBN-13: 978-0692703366
ISBN-10: 0692703365

To my parents and brother, without whom I would know even less about football.

Chapter One

Megan spread the comforter over her bed in her new room and collapsed on top of it, one arm thrown over her eyes. She kicked off her shoes and let out a deep sigh. It was only three in the afternoon and she was already so tired. She and Abby had moved out of their shared apartment so Abby could move in with Lance.

Things had moved fast once Abby and Lance had decided to move in together. They found an available apartment a couple of days after Lance came back and moved in less than a week later. Matt, one of Lance's roommates, had suggested that Megan take Lance's room. It seemed like an easy and convenient solution for everyone, so she'd agreed.

It was definitely going to be an interesting year. She'd need to stop by the tutoring center to rearrange her work schedule now that she lived farther from campus. She had set up her class and work schedule so she had a break in the middle of the day, but she was too far to make the trip home worthwhile, so she'd work during that break and come home earlier in the evenings.

At least she'd gotten Abby's comforter out of the deal. Abby had given it to her right before they'd left their old apartment. She'd said it was the least she could do since she'd left Megan to scramble for a new place to live and forced her to move in with Chris and Matt. Plus, she knew how much Megan loved it and had used it most of the summer. Megan rolled over and snuggled into the comforter, smiling at the memory, too hot still to get underneath. It was so snuggly and cozy. Way better than the quilts she'd used before.

A knock on her open door had her lifting her head and looking over her shoulder. Chris stood in the doorway, letting his hands hang from the top of the door frame by his fingertips. His stance caused his t-shirt to raise a little, a strip of tanned skin on display above the waistband of his shorts that hung off his hips just right.

A frisson of arousal skittered down Megan's spine as her eyes wandered up Chris's form. She resisted the urge to lick her lips. They were roommates now, so she needed to tamp down her attraction. Giving in would be a surefire way to mess up their living arrangements. She didn't want to do that, especially not the day she moved in. "What's up?"

Chris's hazel eyes finished their perusal of her sprawled body and came to rest on her face. She watched his Adam's apple bob while he swallowed and then his tongue came out to run along his lower lip. "Hmm?"

She raised her eyebrows and rolled over so she could sit up. That was an interesting reaction from him. "Did you need something?"

"What? Oh, yeah." Chris dropped his arms and leaned against the doorjamb, his eyes on her face now. "One of our teammates is having a pool party at his parents' house tonight. Matt and I are both going. Wanna come?"

"It's not just for the team?"

Chris lifted one shoulder. "The team and invited guests."

"Sure. You know I'm always up for a party." She shot him a cheeky grin.

He smiled back. "Great. We'll take my car since we won't all fit in Matt's truck. You hungry? We can order pizza or hit a drive-thru before we head to Bryant's."

Megan's stomach let out an audible growl. She laughed. Perfect timing. "Uh, yeah. I could eat. Pizza's fine or grabbing something on the way. Whatever you guys want to do. I'm easy."

Chris's smile grew wider, and a mischievous glint entered his eyes. "You are, huh? That's good to know."

Megan got off the bed. "Yup. I'm easy when it comes to food." She walked over to Chris and patted his chest, stretching up on tiptoe so she could bring her mouth close to his ear, just to mess with him a little. He leaned his head down in response, one corner of his mouth curled up and his breath came faster. "Just food."

She went back on flat feet and pushed at his chest. "If we're going to a party, I want to shower first. I'm all sticky and sweaty from moving."

She stood close enough to see Chris's eyes darken, and his Adam's apple bob again. "Right. Well, I'll leave you to it then. Come out when you're done and we'll figure out food." He straightened and stepped back out into the living room.

Megan closed the door behind him and paused a moment before heading for the shower. Huh. That whole exchange was unexpected.

Chris had started flirting with her when they'd met at the Fourth of July party, but it hadn't progressed beyond that. She would have to be careful about how things played out, though. When she'd decided to move in she hadn't thought it would be a big deal to live with the two football players. They were attractive, sure, but Matt reminded her of her older brothers. And her flirtation with Chris hadn't seemed like anything to take seriously. He flirted with everyone, and she'd seen how they treated Abby, whistling at her and doing everything they could to try to make her blush or make Lance act jealous. She had figured his flirting was just an extension of that.

But the way Chris had looked at her made her wonder if it wasn't more than that after all.

Megan threw on a t-shirt and cut-off denim shorts over the top of her favorite two-piece bathing suit. She figured the red halter-style top with little white polka dots in a vintage pin-up style would be perfect. It was cute and sexy, but wouldn't have a wardrobe malfunction in a pool full of guys. She stuffed a change of clothes, a towel, and an extra pair of flip flops in a bag and was ready to go.

Matt looked up from his place on the couch when she opened the door and smiled at her, blue eyes twinkling. "Roomie!" Megan laughed and stepped closer to the couch. He took in her outfit and backpack. "Ready for the party?"

Megan nodded. "Thanks for letting me tag along."

Matt stood. "Of course. What kind of roommates would we be if we abandoned you on your first night with us?" Megan couldn't help but admire the fit of his board shorts and the t-shirt that skimmed over his well-defined torso. He looked like a surfer with his longish, messy blond hair, Hawaiian print board shorts, and the tribal tattoo peeking out from under his shirt sleeve. He might act like he was her older brother, but that didn't mean she couldn't notice how attractive he was.

"You guys ready?" Chris's voice came from behind her. Megan turned around in time to see him pull on a t-shirt, hiding what looked very much like a six-pack. He wore a pair of blue board shorts with the Captain America shield on the left side. When Megan dragged her eyes back to his face, Chris gave her a knowing smirk. She rolled her eyes, covering her embarrassment at being caught checking him out with a show of disdain. His grin only grew wider.

Matt stood watching their interplay, his eyes bouncing back and forth between them. When Megan turned to face him, he raised an eyebrow at her.

"What?"

He chuckled, shaking his head. "Nothing. Let's go."

He turned and headed for the front door, and Megan followed behind him. When she got to the door she stopped and turned around to crash into Chris's chest. With her nose even with his sternum, the spicy scent of his cologne filled her senses. She fought back the urge to breathe deeper. She looked up at him. "Sorry. I forgot my keys."

He smiled and Megan's eyes locked on his lips. They looked soft and kissable. Before she could think more about that he turned her around and ushered her through the door. "We're all going together. Matt and I both have keys. I promise we won't lock you out."

Megan decided to cover her attraction and embarrassment with arrogance again. "Right. You better not, or you'll be sorry."

Matt and Chris both laughed. Matt held the passenger door open for her to Chris's Chevy Impala. She moved some napkins and a couple of protein bar wrappers off the seat before she climbed in.

Matt took the trash out of her hand and rolled his eyes. "Dude, clean out your car," he called to Chris before climbing in the back seat.

Chris just shrugged. "Oops."

It took about twenty minutes to get to the house on the south side of town after stopping at a drive-thru to get some dinner on the way there. Megan passed most of the ride in silence, watching out the window, listening to Chris and Matt talk about the upcoming football season and what the fall semester was going to look like.

When they arrived at the party there were shirtless football players everywhere. Megan was mesmerized by the various shades of skin tones. It seemed like the full range of colors were laid out before her, from milky white on the guys with farmer's tans, various shades of golden brown and bronze, a couple people with sunburns, to several examples of darker browns.

Megan had always been fascinated by the different shades that existed, thinking how she would blend her oils or pastels to bring out the highlights and shadows on a particular person. The models for her figure drawing classes were almost always white girls. She considered it a treat when she got to see different shades and try to paint them. Maybe that should be her project for this semester's art class—a study of different skin tones in the same set of poses. Her excitement built as she thought about it more. Matt and Chris might even be able to help her convince some of their teammates to pose for her. A range of hot, shirtless football players posing for her wouldn't be a bad project for this semester from any angle she could see.

"Enjoying the view?" Chris's low voice rumbled in her ear and caught her off guard. She whipped her head around, her gaze colliding with his. His brows were pulled down in a scowl. Maybe scratch the idea of trying to get his help. She looked past him to see Matt watching them again, his face bland.

She cleared her throat. "What are you talking about?"

One corner of his mouth turned up, but it wasn't a nice smile. "You're staring, Megan. Are you going to start drooling next?"

It was Megan's turn to scowl. She compressed her lips and lowered her brows to match his. Not wanting to explain her real thoughts, she went with a secondary truth. "I was just seeing if I saw anyone I know. You're not the only football players I've ever met, you know."

Chris didn't say anything, and Megan took a step back to put a little more space between them. Matt angled himself into the space she'd left. "Come on. I'll show you where we're stashing our stuff and give you a tour before we get in the pool. There'll be food later, but we usually start off in the water." She saw him cast an unreadable look back at Chris as he ushered her inside.

Chris stood off to one side of the pool deck and watched the crowd mill around and drank a beer. It was a cheap brand, but that was what you got at a big party. No keg today, just a bunch of cans in coolers full of ice. You don't want glass around the pool, after all.

"Watkins!"

He lifted his chin in greeting to Sullivan, one of his teammates. "Hey."

Sullivan made his way through the crowd, a couple of bikini-clad girls close behind him. "Have you met Brianna and Sarah?" He wrapped his arm around the blonde named Sarah, while Brianna, the redhead, stood off to one side. Both girls had drinks in their hands and flirted with him with their eyes over the tops of their cups. Brianna's eyes roamed over his naked torso with appreciation, and he couldn't help looking her over in return. Her bright bikini top almost couldn't contain her large breasts. The bottoms tied on the sides, meaning it was designed for easy removal.

He nodded at the girls. "I'm Chris." Brianna smiled and stepped closer to him. Sullivan started talking about something, but Chris was distracted by the sight of Megan walking out of the house with Matt. Matt had his arm around her shoulders, and they were laughing together. Chris's mouth went dry when she turned in his direction, and he got his first view of her in her bikini.

Chris interrupted whatever conversation was going on around him. "I'll catch you guys later. I gotta go do something."

He stepped past Sullivan and the girls and headed toward Megan and Matt. He had to suppress the urge to growl at the fact that Matt was touching her. He shouldn't feel jealous. He had no claim to her, but there it was.

The laughter died on Megan's face when she saw him approach. For some reason that pissed him off even more. Matt was eyeing him the same way he had been since they were getting ready to go, and he let his arm slide off Megan's shoulders. "Hey, Chris. What's up?"

"Nothin'. You guys get drinks?"

Megan shook her head. "I wanted to get in the pool before I start drinking."

Matt smiled down at her. She looked so tiny standing there between the two of them. The top of her head was just about even with his armpit. Matt was a little shorter than him, but not much.

"Cool. I'll go in with you." Chris drained the rest of his beer, tossed the can toward a nearby trashcan, and let his hand fall to her back to guide her toward the pool. Her bare skin felt soft and smooth under his hand. He had to stop himself from caressing her and turning the gesture into something more intimate. She cast a glance over her shoulder at Matt, but went along with him without protest. Good.

Chris hopped into the shallow end and turned to help Megan in. She sat down on the edge and put her feet in, hesitating for a moment before accepting his help off the edge. His hands bracketed her waist and her hands went to his shoulders as he lowered her into the water. He knew she didn't need the help, but wanted an excuse to touch her again. Once she was in the pool he forced himself to let go, even though he wanted to keep his hands on her, stake a claim on her, let the others know that she was off limits. But he didn't, and they walked toward the deeper water, closer to the rest of the group in the pool. More girls sat ringing the edge with their feet dangling in the water. "Who's up for a chicken fight?" one of them yelled.

Chris turned toward Megan. "Want to do it?" She looked up at him, her lower lip between her teeth. He almost groaned. "C'mon. It'll be fun." He didn't give her a chance to protest, just grabbed her hand and dragged her over to where the others were already pairing off. Guys disappeared under the water to let their female partners climb on their shoulders.

Chris looked at Megan. "Ready?" She nodded. Without letting go of her hand, he squatted down with his back to her and helped guide her onto his shoulders. Her legs came around the back of his neck, over his shoulders, and she hooked her ankles behind his back. She got on like a pro. She'd obviously done this before. He held onto her hands while he slowly stood, helping her keep her balance. He could feel the muscles in her thighs working to help her steady herself. He stood still for a moment until they both felt stable, then let go to rest his hands on her legs just above her knees. Again he had to stop himself from running his hands over her thighs, managing to content himself with a short stroke of his thumbs. After that he managed to keep his hands still, trying to be matter-of-fact in the way he touched her.

Tompkins was the one in charge of this. They waited while Sullivan and his blonde, whose name Chris had already forgotten, hopped into the pool to join in. Tompkins yelled, "Go!" and they were all at each other.

Chris waded into the fray. Megan grabbed at the shoulder of a brunette on top of one of the linebackers.

She caught her by surprise when the other girl wasn't looking and easily pulled her off. Chris smiled at Megan's cry of triumph before he moved on to find their next opponent. Megan grappled with three other girls, winning each time, before she got taken out by Sullivan's blonde.

Sullivan waited until his girl got a good grip on Megan's arms and stepped backward as fast as he could in the water. It was enough that Megan lost her balance and Chris couldn't keep her upright with the other chick dragging Megan down by her arms.

She came up laughing, pushing her hair out of her face and wiping the water out of her eyes. She splashed water at his chest. "You let me fall off!"

He grinned down at her. "I couldn't help it! You got taken out."

She poked out her lower lip in a fake pout that only lasted a second before she smiled again. "We're supposed to be a team. That means we go down together. Aren't football players supposed to understand the importance of teamwork?"

"Are you questioning my loyalty?" She laughed at him, and he grinned back, his eyes on her mouth. Her lips were plump and red, begging to be kissed. He loved the way she looked, her hair wet and slicked back, her face lit up with a smile.

"It looks like they're going again. Do you want to keep playing?"

Megan's voice pulled his attention back from his wandering thoughts. Giving in to his lust with her was probably a bad idea. Unless maybe she was interested too ...

"Chris?"

"Hmm?"

She gestured at the others. "Are we going to play again?"

Man, she was distracting. He nodded once and grinned. "Let's go."

He dropped down again and she climbed back on. He suppressed a sigh as he realized this was the closest he was going to get to feeling her thighs around his head, and it wasn't from the direction he wanted. But she was his roommate. He needed to remember that.

They played two more rounds of chicken fight. They lost the next round early but won the one after that. Megan sat on his shoulders with her arms raised. "Whoo! We won!"

He laughed, then maneuvered her so she turned and slid down his front. They were pressed together for a moment, her breasts squished against his torso, the bare skin of her belly against his lower abdomen. Megan looked up into his face, and he saw her brown eyes get darker. He dropped his eyes to her lips. They were parted on an indrawn breath, and he wanted to kiss them so bad.

She broke the spell of the moment, stepping back, breaking the contact between them, and he immediately missed the feel of her body pressed against his. "Thanks. I had fun." She glanced over her shoulder toward the shallow end, then looked back at him. "I'm, um. I'm going to go get a drink."

She made her way to the edge and hopped out. Chris waited for her to get out before he followed behind her to get a drink, too.

When he got out of the pool Matt casually approached, a beer in one hand. He walked next to Chris for a few steps before he turned and stepped in front of him. His move forced Chris to stop and looked for all the world like it wasn't intentional, but Chris knew him well enough to know Matt was trying to handle him. Matt's eyes were amused, but he wasn't smiling. He leaned against the low wall that separated the main patio from the pool area, taking a drink of his beer. "What are you doing?"

Chris gestured toward the open door into the house. "Getting a drink."

"Oh, is that all?" Matt's eyebrows went up and he took another sip of his beer. "You sure about that?"

"What's your point, Matt?" Chris wasn't in the mood for this.

Matt shrugged. "Just looks like you're trying to put the moves on our roomie."

"So?"

Matt shook his head. "Bad idea, man." His eyes scanned the party spread out over the yard and in the pool. "There's a whole group of chicks to fuck here, most of them happy to have an hour with you. Leave Megan alone." The amusement had bled out of his eyes as he took another drink of his beer, his stance still casual, but his face and his tone serious.

Chris took a breath, puffing out his chest, unconsciously clenching his fists and flexing his arms. "What if she doesn't want to be left alone?"

Matt just shook his head again. "She's living with us. Use your big head for once instead of your little one."

Chris bristled. Having been classed as a dumb jock all his life, he was sensitive to having his intelligence questioned. "I'm not a fucking idiot."

"I know, man. Didn't say you were. But think about what'll happen if you fuck her. You think she's going to stick around and watch you fuck your way through all these jersey chasers for the rest of the year?" He shook his head again. "Nope. Not that one. She'd hate you and move out at the first opportunity. It was pure dumb luck that she agreed to take Lance's place so we weren't left in the lurch. You really want to fuck that up already?"

Chris clenched his jaw, not wanting to admit that Matt was right, but knowing he was. "You just cockblocking so you can have a shot?"

Matt laughed at that. "Nah. She reminds me too much of my sister. But I like her. She's fun to hang around with and I don't want to pick up her share of the rent until we find another roommate if you fuck her over. You get me?"

Chris deflated a little, relaxing. "Yeah, man. I get you."

Matt nodded once, straightening up. "Good." Chris watched him wander off, still drinking his beer.

Fuck. After feeling her against him, staying away from Megan was going to be harder than he thought. But Matt was right. Fucking her would be a bad idea.

Chapter Two

Megan glanced behind her when she got to the door. Matt and Chris were talking by the edge of the patio. Matt looked relaxed and unconcerned, but Chris was all flexing muscles and narrowed eyes. She couldn't hear them from this distance over the noise of the party, so she wasn't sure what that was about. She wasn't sure if she wanted to find out either.

Instead of getting a drink, she decided to change into dry clothes first. She grabbed her bag from the corner behind the armchair where Matt had stashed their stuff, trying to be quick so she didn't drip all over everything.

She found an empty bathroom where she dried off and changed into her favorite party top and cutoff shorts. It had spaghetti straps and a v-neck that showed off the perfect amount of cleavage. It skimmed over her curves without clinging, just hinting at what was beneath, so that the look was effortless and sexy. She slipped on her favorite wedge sandals and stuffed her flip flops back in her bag along with her swimsuit rolled in her towel.

When she came out of the bathroom, the music had been turned on and people were starting to dance in the clear space on the patio. Megan loved to dance, especially after she'd had a few drinks. She stashed her bag behind the chair again and made her way to the kitchen.

The guy behind the bar lifted his chin at her and smiled when she made her way into his line of sight. "Can I get you something?"

She smiled back, the artist part of her brain noticing the contrast of his white teeth against his dark skin and wondering how she would render that on a canvas. Growing up in a predominately white town meant that she didn't have that much experience painting other skin colors, and her fingers itched for a brush. She pushed those thoughts aside to answer his question. "Whaddaya got?"

He leaned onto the counter on his forearms. "Oh, a little of this, a little of that. Beer, soda, liquor. Want me to mix you something?"

"A Jack and Coke, thanks."

He nodded and snagged a red Solo cup from the stack off to the side, filling it with ice and pouring the soda and whisky into it. When he started to straighten the bottle up after a couple glugs of whisky, she reached out and tipped the bottom back up, letting more liquor pour into her cup. He looked at her and smiled.

"I'm late getting started. I have to catch up." She took the cup from him and took a long drink.

"Well, why don't you stay right here, and I'll help you." He gestured to a bar stool across from him. "I'm Cooper."

"Megan." She slid into the seat, leaning over the bar and drinking some more. It was strong, almost half Jack. Just the way she liked it. She'd seen the cans of Rolling Rock around. It was a popular party beer, but she wasn't a fan. She was snobby about her beer anyway. Hopefully the guys kept good beer in the house.

Cooper mixed himself a drink and apparently decided to give up bartender duties, because he pulled a stool close to hers and sat down. They chatted, and Megan started to enjoy herself more, the warm feeling from the alcohol spreading through her letting her relax. After she'd drained the last of her drink, she slammed the cup down on the counter and grabbed Cooper by the hand. "Let's dance."

He didn't resist, just followed behind her until they were in the small open area where people were dancing. He slid in behind her, one hand on her hip, and moved with her to the beat. They danced together for a couple of songs, then he vanished. Megan stopped dancing and looked behind her, at a loss. She'd thought they were having a nice time. He'd had his hands on her hips and stroking around her waist not that long ago. Now he was nowhere to be seen.

Matt approached with a drink in each hand. "Thirsty?" He held out a cup to her. She frowned up at him, but decided that another drink sounded good. It was another Jack and Coke, nice and strong, just the way she liked it. She moved off the dance floor, hanging with Matt for a while, drinking and chatting. More people joined them, team members and the girls hanging around them. Some of them were girlfriends, some of them were just football player groupies. She'd heard the guys refer to them as jersey chasers, which made her wonder how she was categorized. She wasn't a girlfriend, but she definitely wasn't a jersey chaser.

Not that she'd necessarily turn down any of the hot guys that she got to ogle today, but she wasn't here just to try to get banged by a football player. She was the female roommate of two of the seniors on the team. That apparently put her in a category all her own.

After she finished her drink someone else asked her to dance. Again, after a few songs, he was gone. When she stopped to look around, Chris raised his drink at her and lifted an eyebrow. She nodded. She definitely needed to get more drunk if she couldn't keep a guy dancing with her for more than two or three songs.

Chris met her on her way off the dance floor with another drink, handing it to her, watching her take a long drink. "Having fun?" His eyes glittered with some unreadable emotion.

She gave him a quizzical look. "Um, yeah. Or I would be if my dance partners didn't keep bailing."

Chris just gave a "hmm," in response and buried his face in his cup. Megan couldn't figure out what his deal was tonight. He kept acting strangely. Like he was annoyed with her or something. But he'd been the one to invite her, and when they were in the pool, he hadn't seemed to be bothered by her being there. If he didn't seem so annoyed the rest of the time, she'd think he was attracted to her by the way he insisted she partner with him for the chicken fight, the way he ran his hands over her thighs while she sat perched on his shoulders, and the way he held her against him when he let her down at the end. But he'd been distant since then and was giving her weird looks now. He wasn't even keeping up the easy flirtation they'd started over the summer. She had no idea what she could've done to irritate him. Maybe he felt like her being at the party was cramping his style? Then why did he invite her in the first place? She could've gone to another party by herself, or just stayed home and unpacked and gone to bed early.

"Wanna dance?" Chris's low voice near her ear sent shivers down her spine and pulled her out of her thoughts. She looked up at his face, gauging his sincerity.

"Sure."

He led her by the hand back onto the dance floor. He was still shirtless, his shorts hanging low off his hips, giving her a full view of his defined muscles. The football team had been training and practicing for weeks now, and he was at peak condition. With one hand around her back, he pulled her close, and she could feel the heat he threw off. His smell, a spicy mix of cologne and him, filled her nose. She looked up at his face and his lips curved up in a small smile, his eyes darkening.

Megan's lips parted, her breath coming a little faster at the undisguised desire on Chris's face. She could feel him hardening against her belly where he held her pressed against him.

This time she saw it when Matt pulled Chris away from her. He tapped Chris on the shoulder, and Chris turned, the look on his face morphing to annoyance. He let go of her to face Matt and pushed her behind him. She took a step to the side and watched, surrounded by gyrating bodies, unable to hear them over the music. Matt had an unreadable look on his face. He leaned in, said something close to Chris's ear, and shook his head. Chris's shoulders slumped, he cast a glance over his shoulder at her, his eyes hard, and walked away in the direction of the kitchen.

She watched Chris walk away before turning to Matt. "What was that about?"

He looked down at her and hitched up one side of his mouth in a crooked smile. "Nothin'. Another drink?"

His face didn't give anything away. She agreed with a shrug, and they made their way back to the kitchen. Chris was nowhere to be found, which seemed strange to her since he'd headed this way. Matt stayed with her at the bar until she wandered off in search of a more comfortable place to sit. She found a spot on a couch in the living room. The house had an open floor plan, so she could see into the kitchen as well as out the open patio doors to the pool area. The party was in full swing around her. People were drinking, dancing, making out, having fun.

She wasn't having fun anymore. Her dance partners kept disappearing, and after the way Chris and Matt kept showing up with drinks just as she found herself alone combined with their little performance on the dance floor, she had the sneaking suspicion they were responsible for that. She couldn't figure out what Chris's deal was. He acted like he wanted her, but then he kept shutting down. It was probably for the best that way. She just wished he wouldn't go to the trouble of making her seem off-limits to everyone else if he wasn't going to follow through.

She looked up and saw Chris across the room, a redhead hanging off him, her hands all over his arms and chest. Not long after that it looked like they were having a competition to see whose tongue could go further down the other's throat. She tore her eyes away, not wanting to see any more of that.

Chris pulled away from the redhead—Brianna?—who'd just given him a taste of what she'd been drinking. Something sweet and fruity from what he could tell. She ran a hand up his chest. "Should we find an empty bedroom?"

He looked toward the living room just in time to see Megan turn her head away from his direction. Damn. Any thought he had of getting laid tonight vanished. He shook his head, taking the girl's hands off his chest. "Thanks for the offer, but not tonight."

She turned her head to follow the direction of his gaze. She snorted. "Have fun with that." Chris turned his gaze to her, hearing the bite in her tone. He didn't like it when girls got catty, especially over him. It's not like he was trying to find a girlfriend by sleeping with some random chick at a party. He never even remembered their names once he was done, sometimes before he even got started. What was the point of acting jealous and possessive of a one-night stand?

"On second thought, not ever." He dropped her hands and went into the kitchen. He needed another drink. These pool parties were usually fun. It was a great way for the team to blow off steam together before the season started. They were done with two-a-day practices since classes started on Monday and their first game was next weekend. The next few months were busy, with only one Saturday off between now and Thanksgiving. The annual pool party before classes started cemented the bond the team formed during the preseason practices and got them game-ready. But Chris wasn't feeling it this year.

Matt found him at the bar, downing a few more shots. He wore a frown. "I thought you were the DD tonight, man."

Chris knocked back another shot of tequila and shrugged. "Plans change."

Matt crossed his arms. "Don't you think you ought to tell the other potential drivers if you need to change plans?"

"Fuck off, Schwartz. You've been in my face enough tonight. You can sober up enough to drive in an hour or two if you stop drinking now." He gestured toward the living room. "Or tell Megan to stop drinking so she can drive." He poured himself another shot and drank it in one swallow, barely feeling the burn of the liquor anymore. Normally when he'd had this many shots he had a nice buzz going and a warm feeling of contentment centered in his chest. Now he was just pissed. In more ways than one. He was angry and drunk and the alcohol wasn't doing anything to make him feel better.

He raised his eyes to Matt's face. Matt made a sound of disgust and headed for the living room. Chris figured he was going to talk to Megan, but he didn't care to watch. The two of them seemed closer than he liked. He didn't see her giving Matt the same searching or wary looks she shot at him. And Matt had been touching her off and on all night long. Way more than he had. He'd only touched her under the guise of playing a game, and then for the one time they'd danced together before Matt interrupted them.

The more he thought about it, the more pissed off he became. At Matt. At Megan. At the whole fucking situation. And he wasn't even going to be able to get laid, because he kept seeing the look on Megan's face when he'd looked up from kissing that other chick. It was a mixture of hurt and disgust.

Fuck that. What right did she have to be hurt or disgusted? He was a man. He had needs. This was a party. She hadn't been disgusted when she'd been dancing with his teammates and they'd had their hands all over her ass. What right did she have to be disgusted with him? They'd just been kissing. It wasn't like he was fucking her against the wall in front of everyone. Which sometimes happened at these parties. Not that he would do that. He wasn't an exhibitionist. But other guys didn't seem to care if anyone saw them.

He'd been planning on getting laid tonight. He didn't want the redhead anymore. She seemed like she could turn into a clingy bitch, and that was the last thing he needed. Someone else, though. There was always a whole crowd of jersey chasers at these things. Surely he could find one to take care of him for tonight.

Chapter Three

A shaft of light from the split in the curtains fell across Megan's face. She groaned and rolled over, her head pounding. The familiar roiling in her stomach had her lurching out of bed and stumbling into the bathroom, where she heaved up whatever was left in her stomach.

She sank onto the floor in the unfamiliar bathroom. A wan smile crossed her face. *Breaking in the new digs.* She was christening her new bathroom with her first hangover. It had taken much longer to do this in the apartment she'd shared with Abby. She'd always felt a little bad about leaving Abby at home by herself when they'd lived together. Partly because she'd felt like she was abandoning Abby, despite Abby's protestations that she liked staying home and reading or watching a movie or whatever it was she did while Megan was out partying. Partly because she'd always thought Abby needed to break out of her shell a little more.

And she'd been right. Except it had been a guy that had done what she'd begun to think was impossible. Megan felt justified in taking some credit. She was the one that had dragged Abby to the party where she'd met Lance. And she'd helped push them together a little bit along the way, encouraging Abby to give Lance a chance, even when Abby kept insisting it couldn't be anything serious. The best part had been organizing their reunion. When Lance had called her to get her help, she'd jumped up and down and had to avoid Abby for hours afterward so Abby didn't think she was crazy because she couldn't stop smiling.

She was so happy for Abby. Sad for herself since she wasn't living with her best friend anymore, but happy for her friend to find someone that cared about her and wasn't afraid to show it. Who wouldn't be easily pushed away and wouldn't bail like the other men in Abby's life had.

Thinking about Abby and Lance had her feeling so happy that she forgot for a second that she had a splitting headache. She got up off the floor. And immediately regretted it when the room spun and her head felt like it was filled with cement. She let out a groan with a hand on her forehead, her pulse pounding in her temples.

A soft knock sounded at her bedroom door. "Megan? Can I come in?" It was Matt.

She stumbled to the door, opened it wide enough to lean in the opening, and gave him her signature hangover death glare. He grinned down at her and held up a glass of water. "I have water and ibuprofen. I thought you could use it."

Megan eased up on the death glare and opened the door further so she could take the water and painkillers. She eyed him over the top of her cup after throwing the pills in her mouth. His blond hair was messy, but that wasn't unusual. He didn't look all that bleary eyed. She took a few swallows, making sure the pills didn't get caught in her throat. Then drank some more to get the residual vomit taste out of her mouth. "Thanks. How come you're so chipper?"

Matt shrugged and leaned against the doorframe, crossing his arms. His pecs and biceps bulged in full view, the tattoo on his right arm looking like it was rippling. He wasn't wearing a shirt. "I didn't get shit-faced last night."

His voice dragged Megan's eyes off his naked torso. He was grinning at her, his blue eyes twinkling. She took another drink of water. "You didn't? I thought Chris was supposed to be the DD."

"Yeah. He was. He changed his mind, and since you were already well on your way to completely trashed, I got the job instead."

Megan realized that water couldn't take care of the taste in her mouth and gestured Matt into her room. She went into the bathroom and got out her toothbrush. The water was helping her feel a little more alive already, and soon the ibuprofen would kick in, dulling the throbbing of her head. A minty fresh mouth would only make things better. She spread some toothpaste on the brush and stuck it in her mouth before standing in the doorway. "'Splain."

Matt's grin grew wider. "There's not much else to explain. Chris got pissed about something and started drinking shots of tequila like water. I'd only had a few beers at that point, and I don't know how many drinks you'd had, but if they were all as strong as you like, you'd had quite a bit by then. Don't you remember me making you alternate with water after a while?"

Megan thought back to the night before. A vague recollection of her drunkenly telling Matt how he was ruining all her fun filtered into her memory. Heat prickled up her neck and over her cheeks. "Um, yeah. I think I remember something about that."

Matt laughed. "I don't think I've ever seen you blush before. I didn't know you had it in you."

Megan flipped him off. "Don't get used to it. It doesn't happen often."

He just laughed again. "No worries. You're an entertaining drunk. Which is better than I can say for Chris. He was a moody drunk last night. He's usually not that bad."

"Yeah. He seemed off to me too." She ducked back into the bathroom to spit and rinse out her mouth.

When she came back out, Matt was standing. "We always get breakfast burritos from this little place that serves them all day. Let me know what you want and I'll bring you one."

"Sure. Thanks."

"Cool. Come on out whenever. Chris is still in bed, so he won't bother you."

"Thanks."

He nodded and walked out of her bedroom, closing the door behind him. It was nice of Matt to try to make her feel welcome. He seemed to have decided to take on the role of protector where she was concerned. Including her in what he and Chris were doing, making sure she drank water at the party last night, keeping overeager guys away from her, bringing her hangover remedies and food this morning. He was a good guy.

If Chris could just get with that program, living here wouldn't be too bad.

Chris drifted out of the athletic center on his way to his first class. Maybe the last time ever he'd be going to his first class. Not because he'd be graduating in December—that was out of the question—but because he might not bother coming back in the spring. He was only here still so he could play his last season.

When Megan had mentioned that she worked as a tutor it made him wonder if she could help him manage to graduate. Part of the reason he was considering just quitting once the semester was over was because he wasn't even sure if he'd be able to graduate in May. Maybe if he actually tried. But that meant he needed to care. That was the real sticking point.

As if thinking of her had conjured her up, Megan appeared in front of him. She came out of a building he'd never been in on the other side of the grass from him. From this angle he couldn't see the name of the building, so he had no idea what it was. She was looking down at something in her hands and hadn't noticed him watching from the sidewalk across the way.

A guy came out behind her and said something to her. He was too far away to hear, but it obviously wasn't nice. Megan stiffened, and she turned to face the newcomer. Even in profile Chris could tell she was pissed. Their exchange got more heated.

Chris wanted to step in, but he didn't know if his help would be welcome. Megan had avoided them yesterday, leaving the house and staying gone for hours. Not that he had any room to complain. He'd done the same thing the day before. Matt had kept her company all day, which irritated Chris. He'd wanted to try to talk to her, but not with Matt sitting next to her on the couch.

Just because their home life was starting out awkwardly didn't mean he wanted to see some guy getting her riled up. He wanted to rile her up, and not in the way this guy was doing. He'd decided to leave her alone, but that didn't mean he should let her fend for herself against assholes when he could do something about it.

Decision made, he hitched his backpack higher on his shoulder and started across the grass, his free hand clenched in a fist at his side. The guy that was bothering Megan looked up and his eyes widened a little before his normal, arrogant look returned to his face. He said one more thing in Megan's ear, low enough that Chris still couldn't hear, and walked off.

Megan turned to face him, still looking mad. He lifted a hand, about to reach out for her to offer some kind of comfort but let it drop. He shouldn't touch her. "Are you okay?"

"Yeah. Fine."

He snorted. "Really? 'Cause you don't sound fine. Who was that?" He looked in the direction that the asshole had gone.

"Isaac." Megan's voice was tight, and her feelings about Isaac were clear.

"Ex-boyfriend?"

"God, no. Not for lack of trying, though." He raised his eyebrows at that. She noticed and let out a laugh, but it sounded mean, not her usual full laugh that he really liked. "On his part, not mine. I thought I made that clear over the summer, but he doesn't like to take no for an answer."

Chris didn't like the sound of that. He looked her over again. Her face was relaxing a little and she looked less pissed off. She didn't look close to tears, which was good. If that asshole had made her cry, he'd have to find him and make him cry. "Okay. If he keeps bothering you, let me know."

Megan laughed again, this one a little more genuine sounding. "Thanks. That's sweet, but completely unnecessary."

She turned to go in the opposite direction of where he was headed. Chris stopped her with a hand on her arm. "I'm serious. If he keeps bothering you like that, tell me. Or if you don't want to tell me, at least tell Matt. You don't need assholes treating you like that."

Megan narrowed her eyes. "How much did you hear?"

"Nothing. I could tell by your reactions that it wasn't a nice chat with an old friend. If he's bothering you, we'll make sure he decides it's in his best interest not to."

Megan maintained eye contact, and they were frozen like that for a minute—eyes boring into each other, his hand gripping her bicep. He wasn't going to back down on this, though, and she needed to know that. He and Matt looked out for their own, and whatever else was going on, she was their roommate and best friends with Lance's girl. She was part of their group now, whether she liked it or not.

She broke first, dropping her eyelids and stepping back so they weren't touching anymore. "Okay. Fine. He's harmless, though. All talk."

"All talk? What kind of talk? What did he actually say to you?"

Megan looked him in the eye again. "Nothing important. I promise I'll tell you if he keeps bothering me." She checked the time on her phone. "I have a class. I'll see you at home."

He nodded and watched her walk away until she got out of sight. He finally turned and walked to his own class. His palm tingled where he'd touched her skin. Matt was right. He needed to keep his hands off her if he couldn't fuck her.

Chapter Four

Chris took off his pads, ready for a shower after another hot practice. He looked forward to September and the cooler weather. September and October were perfect for football. Not too hot and not too cold. The night games in October got pretty chilly, but as long as you were playing it wasn't too bad. November was a mixed bag. It could be like October and not be too cold. Or it could be snowy, or raining and thirty-three degrees, which was the worst. There was nothing more miserable than being soaked at nearly freezing temperatures. He'd rather it dropped a few degrees and just turned to snow.

A voice from the next bank of lockers caught Chris's attention. "I'm telling you, dude. She told me she's living with two guys. What I wouldn't give to be one of them."

Chris dropped his jersey and stood up, not moving, waiting to hear more. He wasn't disappointed.

"You think they get up to some kinky shit?" Another voice. Sniggers and laughter followed the question.

"I don't know, man, but I'd love to find out." The first voice again, putting extra emphasis on the word love. More laughter. "Those curls would be perfect for grabbing hold and hanging on."

"How do you know she's not shaved?" A different voice this time, followed by the sound of something hitting a locker.

"I meant the curls on her head, sicko."

"I'm not the one fantasizing about a threesome with another guy!" Another thud of something hitting a locker, followed by more laughter.

"I didn't say anything about a threesome!"

"Why didn't you tap that at the party over the weekend then?"

The first guy made a derisive noise, a combination of a snort and a growl. "Her roommates wouldn't let anyone near her for long enough to get a chance. All the more reason to suspect she's boning both of 'em."

Chris had heard enough. He rounded the corner, fists clenched, ready to beat someone down. A girl at the party with curly hair that lived with two guys? No way they weren't talking about Megan. And the fact that the jackass acknowledged her roommates were protecting her from assholes like him just clinched it.

There were three guys there, two still in their pants and one sitting on the bench with a towel across his lap. He grabbed the guy he assumed was the first speaker and slammed him against the lockers. At least he wasn't the one in the towel. He recognized him as one of the guys that had danced with Megan at the party on Saturday. He was pretty sure he'd seen the guy with his hands all over her ass.

"Dude! What's your problem?" Yup. Chris had the main shit-talker.

"You're my problem." He shoved him into the lockers a little harder, banging the asshole's head again, his left arm barred across the guy's throat, his right hand ready to administer a beating if necessary. He felt another pair of hands pulling at his shoulder, but he didn't pay them any attention.

The asshole's eyes darted around, looking behind Chris. Probably hoping for someone to save him. Chris looked him over. He was some pissant little sophomore that wasn't even a starter yet. He was on defense, but Chris couldn't remember his name. Right now he didn't give a shit.

Chris exerted a little more pressure with his arm until the pissant's eyes returned to his face, bugging out just a little. Chris curved his lips in a menacing smile. "Good. I have your attention." He paused. "If I ever hear you running your mouth about her again, you're not going to be able to talk for a long time afterward." The guy's eyes bulged more while Chris increased the pressure for a second before he let go. He pulled away in disgust and grabbed a spare towel to wipe the other guy's sweat from his arm. The other two guys were staring at him as he tossed the towel back on the bench. "That goes for all of you."

"I don't know what you're talking about, man. We were just—" The little pissant didn't get to finish that sentence. Chris had his arm across his neck again, his head hitting the lockers harder than before.

"You know exactly what I'm talking about. You might be a piece of shit, but there's no way you're that stupid." Chris punched the lockers next to the asshole's head for emphasis. "Leave her alone. Don't touch her. Don't talk to her. Don't talk about her. She's off-limits."

Chris let him go and turned to walk away. "That must be some pussy to make you act like that."

White-hot fury rose up inside Chris. He charged the asshole again, this time intending to knock his teeth into his throat. A pair of hands caught his bicep, keeping his arm back. Another pair grabbed his other arm. Together they pulled him back, away from the asshole who didn't know when to keep his mouth shut. When he was a safe distance away from that little pissant sophomore again, he shook off the guys holding him back. "Not another word about her."

He turned to see Matt give him a questioning look. Matt obviously hadn't heard anything, or else he'd've helped him pound the guy into a pulp instead of holding him back. But it was for the best. He'd be suspended from the first two games for fighting if Matt hadn't intervened.

Chris filled Matt in later, after they were gone and neither of them could give that little asshole the beating he deserved. Matt's face turned thunderous. Good. At least Chris wasn't the only one who wanted to protect Megan. Not that he'd doubted Matt, it was just nice that he wasn't on his own.

"We'll have to keep her away from the parties the team goes to."

Chris nodded. "Definitely. But how do you think we'll manage that?"

One corner of Matt's mouth quirked up in a half smile. It was sad looking, though, and Chris wasn't sure why. "I don't think it'll be too hard. She didn't seem to have as much fun as normal at the party on Saturday. I doubt she'll want to party with us or our teammates again any time soon."

Chris didn't understand. She hadn't had fun? She'd seemed like she was having a good time when they'd played chicken fight and later when she was dancing. With practically everyone. Chris suppressed the growl that was fighting to come out. He hadn't liked seeing her dance with all those guys, watching them put their hands all over where he wanted to touch and couldn't. It was probably best that they wanted to keep her away from the team's parties, because he couldn't handle watching her party like that and not being able to be the one touching her.

Instead of voicing his confusion, Chris just grunted. If Matt was right, it would just make things easier, so he let it go.

Megan settled into the rhythm of the semester within a couple of weeks. Chris and Matt were gone the first two weekends with away games, which made it easy to unpack and settle in and start to feel more at home in her new place. She'd started to get some drop-in clients in the tutoring center. The first papers were starting to be assigned in the English classes, and assignments were getting more difficult. Things would only continue getting harder until finals were over in early December, making people seek out help. She also had a few regular tutoring clients, including Matt, who'd gotten special permission from his coach to use her as his tutor instead of his assigned tutor. He said he had a history with his assigned tutor and didn't feel he'd learn well from her this semester.

Megan stood at the stove chuckling to herself at the memory of Matt telling her about how he'd broken up with his tutor, who he'd dated last year. He was a funny guy, and had a self-deprecating sense of humor that made his antics almost endearing instead of slap-worthy. She still couldn't believe he'd broken up with her by text. What an ass.

On Friday night Megan decided to make dinner. The guys' first home game was this weekend, so she wanted to make sure they got a big dinner full of protein and carbs to see them through tomorrow. She smiled to herself while she whisked together the ingredients for an Alfredo sauce. It would be perfect over the shrimp and chicken on a bed of fettuccine. She used to help her mom do this for her brothers when she was growing up.

The memory of happy times with her mom made her feel a little pang of regret. Her parents wouldn't approve of her living with two guys. They were conservative and religious. With a mental shrug, she pushed the thoughts away. They didn't approve of her life at all since she left home. They thought her art major was frivolous and unsuitable, and they didn't like that she partied. Her relationship with them was strained at the best of times, and her brothers didn't help. They weren't perfect angels, but they put on the front to please their parents and encouraged her to do the same. But Megan couldn't bring herself to lie to her parents. Of all the things she'd been taught growing up, honesty was the thing that stuck. So instead of lying, she just didn't talk to her parents much or go home to visit. In fact, she hadn't been home since last Christmas, even though her parents only lived forty-five minutes away. The lack of contact had prompted her mom to increase her efforts, though. She'd been calling more and more often over the summer, and Megan knew she shouldn't keep ignoring her or only talking for a few minutes when she did answer. She just didn't want to deal with the disapproving silence or the pleas for her to move back home.

The side door slammed shut, alerting her that one of her roommates was home and pulling her out of her thoughts. The sound of the screen slamming again meant both guys were home. Despite all living together and going to the same school, their schedules were different enough that they took separate cars every day.

"It smells good in here."

Megan turned to see Matt coming into the kitchen. She smiled at him. "I hope you guys are hungry. I made dinner." They'd become friends over the last couple of weeks, hanging out together at the house and during their tutoring sessions. He reminded her a lot of Charlie, her middle brother, goofing off and joking around a lot. Chris avoided them for the most part.

Matt laughed. "We're always hungry. Especially after practice." He peered at the stove over her shoulder. "I didn't know you could cook."

"I made brownies for the Fourth of July party."

"Baking's not the same thing." He stuck a finger in the sauce before she could smack him away and stuck it in his mouth. "Mm ... and you're a good cook, too." He winked at her. "I could get used to this."

Megan smacked him on the chest. "Keep your fingers out of the pot. I don't want your dirty hands messing up my food."

"I just washed them, I swear!" Matt held up his hands, his eyes dancing with laughter. Megan laughed along with him. He surprised her by swooping down and giving her a hug, lifting her up off her feet for a second before setting her down again.

A throat cleared in the entrance to the kitchen and they turned to see Chris standing there, arms crossed, muscles bulging, jaw clenched. Matt dropped his hands from her and took a step back. "Hey. Megan's making dinner."

Chris just nodded in response.

"Are you hungry?" Megan tried to keep her voice upbeat, but Chris glowering at her made it difficult. He was acting … jealous? Angry? Was he mad that Matt was touching her? Why? He had no reason to be jealous. For one thing, nothing would ever happen between her and Matt. They were just friends. And for another, nothing was happening with her and Chris. That was out of the question too. The roommate thing meant they couldn't get together. Plus, Chris was more of a manwhore than Lance had been from what she could tell. At least Lance had taken his conquests out to dinner first. It would be unwise to get involved with him given his history and proximity.

Chris just stood watching them, Matt leaning against the counter near the stove. She looked from Chris's stony face to Matt's watchful one and back to the food on the stove. She cleared her throat. "The food's almost ready. Matt, why don't you get bowls for everyone. Chris, will you get us all drinks please?"

She kept her back to them, facing the stove. Matt started getting bowls and silverware right away. It took Chris a little longer, but she eventually heard him opening the refrigerator to get out the pitcher of water they kept in there.

By the time Megan had dished out the food, the tension had mostly drained out of the room. Chris wasn't clenching his jaw as much and engaged in conversation after a few minutes, even answering questions with more than one word. Matt was more subdued than he had been when he first came into the kitchen, his eyes watchful on Chris and on her. Megan tried to keep things light, directing conversation to how classes were going and how they thought the season was shaping up.

"So far we're one and one. We have a bunch of new starters on the offensive line this year. A lot of guys graduated since last year. Or at least they've been in school too long to be eligible to play still. We lost a couple starters because they were academically ineligible. Coach Hanson was pissed when he found out." Megan had to make an effort not to freeze in shock. She didn't think she'd heard more than two or three words at a time come from Chris since she'd moved in.

She nodded in understanding. "So, are you keeping up with your classes pretty well?"

Chris shrugged and mumbled something.

Megan frowned. "Seriously, Chris. Aren't you supposed to graduate in December? Why wouldn't you make sure you're keeping up with your classes?"

He shook his head. "I'm not going to be graduating in December."

"But I thought over the summer you guys said you'd both be done after this semester." Megan looked over to Matt, who looked surprised as well.

Chris shrugged. "I probably will be done after this semester. I just won't be graduating." He shoveled a forkful of pasta into his mouth, clamping his lips shut while he chewed and keeping his head down.

Megan sat stunned, unsure how to respond to that. She looked to Matt again, but he just stared at Chris too, with his fork frozen halfway to his mouth. "Um, well, couldn't you graduate in May, then? It's pretty normal for student athletes to take five years, isn't it?"

Chris didn't respond, not looking up from his plate. She looked at Matt again. He'd managed to get his fork to his mouth and was contemplating Chris while he chewed. Megan did finally manage to catch his eye. He shrugged one shoulder, nodding and swallowing. "Yeah. Five years is pretty normal. I had some transfer credits from dual enrollment in high school. That's why I'm able to graduate in December instead of taking until May."

She turned back to Chris. "If you need help, I can—"

"Drop it." His eyes were on his plate, but his voice was steel.

"But—"

He silenced her with a look, his eyes hard, his voice harder. "I said drop it."

She looked at Matt again and he gave a fractional shake of his head. Megan took a deep breath and looked down at her plate, pushing the remaining food around. Just before she got up to clear her plate, having decided she wasn't hungry anymore, Matt spoke.

"So are you coming to the game tomorrow?"

Megan looked up at him. "Uh, I don't think so. I don't usually go to football games."

"What? You have to come. You're our roommate. Isn't it your job to support us now?"

Megan smirked. "Yeah. I'm your roommate. Not your girlfriend. Would you try to sell me that line of bull if I were a guy?"

Matt nodded. "Probably. But a guy wouldn't make us dinner, so it's a moot point. Come to the game."

Megan was about to beg off again, when Chris spoke up. "You should come." His voice was softer now than it had been. She looked at him. His face was neutral, not telling her anything. He held her gaze and she couldn't look away.

Finally, she nodded. "Alright. I'll come."

Chapter Five

Megan looked up at the bleachers. About halfway up on the right a girl with strawberry blonde hair pulled back into a ponytail jumped up and down while she waved. Megan waved back and made her way up the stairs to where Abby waited. Lance stood up from his seat on the end, towering over both of them, so that Abby could pull Megan into a tight hug.

"I feel like I haven't seen you in forever!" squealed Abby.

Megan squeezed her back before they broke apart. "It's only been a couple weeks, and we've been texting." She moved past Abby to the seat they'd saved for her.

Megan leaned forward so she could look past Abby, letting her gaze roam over Lance. He looked good as always in a Superman t-shirt that stretched across his broad shoulders, the breeze ruffling his dark hair. Abby had lucked out when she scored this one. "Hey, Lance. How's it going?"

He grinned back at her, his dark eyes warm. "Good. You? How's life in my old house?"

"Uh, it's interesting."

Lance laughed. "I bet. They behaving themselves?"

"I guess? I don't see them a whole lot between classes and practices and away games. I see Matt more than Chris because I'm his tutor, but we're almost always talking about class stuff. I don't know what they get up to when I'm not around."

Lance's eyebrows climbed his forehead and a look of speculation entered his dark eyes. "You're tutoring Matt? That's ... interesting. Are you tutoring Chris too?"

She shook her head. "No. Matt wanted me to be his tutor because we have a couple classes together. He convinced the coach to let him work with me instead of the regular tutor because of that and because of his history with the other tutor."

"Huh." Lance didn't say anything else, just looked her over with that same speculation in his eyes before he turned away.

Megan didn't have much time to think about what that look might mean before Abby reclaimed her attention. They chatted about the semester and how classes were going so far. Their paths didn't cross much on campus. Megan was an art major with a marketing minor, and Abby was majoring in Spanish. Not a lot of crossover there.

The one thing that was glaringly obvious was how happy Abby was. Megan hadn't ever seen her like this. Between Abby's mom and her brother's disappearing act a few years ago, Abby had had a lot on her plate without much help. Megan had known Lance would be good for Abby since shortly after they'd started seeing each other over the summer. Seeing her now, you'd never know she had anything weighing her down. She was buoyant and more animated than Megan had ever seen her.

Conversation died down when the game started. They were playing Campbell Christian College, a small school in Oregon. Megan's parents would've preferred that she go there, even though they were happy about how close she'd be to home at first. That is, until she'd moved in with Abby and stopped going to church by the end of the first semester.

Lance cheered throughout the game and she and Abby joined in when it seemed appropriate. They giggled together about everything, since neither of them followed football that much. Megan knew what was going on because she'd grown up watching her brothers play. She hadn't been to a game since high school, though. Once her middle brother graduated after her junior year, she hadn't felt the need to go. Being at a game again made her miss him.

It was fun to see names she recognized on jerseys again, even if they weren't related to her.

It was a close game. At halftime the other team was up by a touchdown. They maintained their lead throughout the second half. But at the end of the fourth quarter, Chris caught an interception. He ran it back, dodging and twisting to keep away from would-be tacklers. Right before he got to the end zone it looked like they were going to get him. A CCC player got ahold of his jersey.

The crowd was on its feet cheering him on. Lance's deeper voice cut through the noise of the crowd, screaming for Chris to keep moving. Megan bounced on the balls of her feet yelling, "Go! Go! Go!" Abby stood between them with a hand clapped over her mouth.

Chris kept going, but he struggled to stay on his feet. It didn't look like he would be able to make the touchdown before he went down. Then Matt came out of nowhere, wrapped his arms around the CCC guy's legs, and took him out. Chris managed to shake free, and ran the last few steps down the field, spiking the ball.

The whole stadium erupted in cheers. Lance was screaming and she and Abby were both jumping up and down, wordless cheers coming from everywhere. The last play of the game was a two point conversion, putting Marycliff ahead. CCC made a valiant effort for a final touchdown, throwing a long Hail Mary pass. The receiver touched the ball with the tips of his fingers, but fumbled it before he could pull it in. Marycliff players covered the ball, taking final possession. When they lined up for the next play, Marycliff took a knee, and the last few seconds on the clock ran out.

Megan was exhilarated by the game. She'd been bored when the score stayed the same for almost two full quarters, but the last five minutes of play had been pure adrenaline.

Lance led them down to wait by the player's entrance so they could catch up with Chris and Matt and some of the other guys. They hung out for a while, waiting for the team to complete their post-game rituals. Soon enough, players started trailing out alone and in small groups. Several of them stopped to talk to Lance. She and Abby recognized a few of the guys from meeting them over the summer at a couple of parties.

Megan waved at Cooper, the guy she'd met at the pool party right before classes started. He stared at her for a long moment before he lifted his chin in return, but didn't approach. His eyes moved to look over her shoulder and she turned her head. Chris loomed over her, his eyes hard and his jaw firm. She looked back at Cooper. His eyes flicked to her and back to Chris, then he turned and walked away.

Megan turned toward Chris, who still watched Cooper's retreating back with the same stony expression. "What was that about?"

Chris waited a beat before he looked down at her. He let out a breath, his puffed-out chest returning to its normal dimensions. He shook his head once. "Nothing."

Before she could push for an actual explanation, he turned away from her and started talking to Lance and Matt. She looked at Abby, who'd watched the entire thing with raised eyebrows.

Their eyes met and Abby stepped closer to her. "What was that?"

Megan looked over at the trio of guys talking and laughing like nothing had happened. They were caught up in the details of the game, congratulating Chris on his interception and touchdown. She shook her head. "I have no idea."

"C'mon, let's go to the bathroom before we head out. I don't think we're going home any time soon and I have to pee." She waved to get Lance's attention and let him know where they were going. He nodded and Abby pulled Megan after her by the arm.

Once they were around the corner and out of earshot Abby stopped and turned to her. "Okay, we haven't talked in awhile. What's going on with you and Chris?"

"Don't you have to pee?"

"Yeah, but not that bad. You normally tell me everything that's going on, and I haven't heard anything about Chris going all macho and possessive around you. Why are you holding out on me? I never thought I'd be the one hounding you for information."

Megan rolled her eyes. "That's because there isn't anything to tell." She started walking again, heading for the bathroom. Abby came along too. "The guy I waved at danced with me at a party the weekend before classes started. The way he reacted, though, it makes me wonder if Matt and Chris scared him off without me realizing it at the time. And I have no idea what that was about back there." She stopped and did her best impression of how Chris had puffed out his chest, then relaxed with a laugh and kept walking.

Abby laughed with her and glanced at her out of the corner of her eye. She pushed open the door to the bathroom and held it for Megan. "Weren't you guys flirting quite a bit over the summer?"

Megan stopped halfway into a stall and narrowed her eyes at Abby's faux-innocent expression. "Yes. What's your point?"

Abby just shrugged and went into her own stall. "No point. Just asking a question."

"Right. No point at all, I'm sure. The answer to your real question is no, nothing's going on there. We flirted over the summer, yeah, but he's barely spoken to me since I've been living there. There's been nothing that could even be remotely construed as flirtatious in any dimension since the day I moved in."

Conversation stopped until they were both washing their hands. Abby looked at Megan in the mirror. "Did something happen on move-in day?"

Megan considered the question for a moment before she answered. Did something happen on move-in day? She couldn't put her finger on anything specific, but it did seem like that was when everything had changed between her and Chris. Their relationship had gone from easy and flirtatious to uncomfortable and barely speaking to one another. She and Matt had gotten closer since then, but Chris was always prickly and monosyllabic whenever they were in the same room for more than a few minutes. It had gotten to where she didn't even try to engage him in conversation anymore, which was why dinner the night before had been so surprising.

She shook the water off her hands and reached for a paper towel, bringing her eyes back to Abby's face. Abby watched her, waiting for an answer to her question. Megan shook her head back and forth while she thought about it. "I can't think of anything, really." She filled Abby in on the basics of what had happened at the pool party, pausing for a second to think before she finished. "Chris got really drunk even though he was supposed to drive, and Matt ended up driving. I don't know what that was all about." She grinned at Abby. "They don't give in to my bullying for information as easily as you."

Abby laughed at that. "They just haven't learned how persistent you can be. Plus, I bet you don't follow them into their bedrooms or the bathroom continuing to pester them until they give in." She arched one blonde eyebrow at Megan.

"True. Chris makes it clear he doesn't want me around. And Matt's like my big brother. I don't want to see him naked. And I have the feeling that if I followed him into the bathroom he'd pee in front of me regardless. You're too shy to do that, so I could always hold you hostage that way when you wouldn't fess up."

"That is one thing I definitely don't miss about living with you."

Megan poked out her lower lip in a fake pout. "You don't miss me?" She sniffed.

Abby just laughed at her. "Of course I miss you. It's weird living with a boy."

It was Megan's turn to laugh. "You practically lived with him all summer."

"I know, but it's different now that it's our place. Before it was his place and I just stayed over. Now I'm actually living with him and we share a bathroom and a kitchen and stuff. I haven't lived in the same house as a guy since Daniel bailed on Mom and me, and he was my brother, so it's not at all the same thing."

Abby pulled out her phone and laughed. "Lance is wondering if we got lost. We should probably head back."

Megan pulled the door open and held it for Abby before she followed her out. She linked her arm in Abby's and laid her head on Abby's shoulder for a moment as they walked. "I know what you mean. It is way different living with guys. I miss being roommates. You're quieter and cleaner and not gone for days at a time for football games. It's weird. I get used to having them around making boy noises all over the house, and then they're gone. I just start getting used to being alone in the house, and then they're back, tromping around, slamming doors, and playing video games till late."

Abby laughed. "I told you it would be weird." She pulled them to a stop so she could look at Megan's face. "You are doing okay, aren't you? You'd tell me if it was too much, right?"

"Yeah, I'm fine. It's only been a few weeks. We're all still adjusting. You're happy with Lance, though, right?"

The grin that split Abby's face was answer enough. Megan tugged on her arm to get her moving again. "Good."

Chapter Six

"Dude, what was that all about?"

Chris pulled his eyes away from the retreating forms of Megan and Abby and turned to Lance. "What was what about?"

Lance just laughed. "You went all possessive caveman around Megan when she waved at that other guy. I didn't recognize him. He new?"

"Yeah. He's a sophomore, I think. It's his first season here."

"Right. And your little show of intimidation? You screwing her or something?"

Chris shoved Lance. "Fuck off, man. It's not like that. That little asshole was talking trash about her in the locker room. I just wanted to make sure he remembers to leave her alone."

Lance just laughed and glanced at Matt, who nodded, confirming Chris's story. "What was he saying?"

Chris clenched his jaw and flexed his hands, trying to keep from making fists again. "I don't want to talk about it."

Lance looked at Matt again, who just shrugged. "I don't know, man. I walked in just in time to stop Chris from breaking the guy's face. I didn't hear what he said, but from what Chris told me it wasn't very flattering to our little roomie. It's probably good I didn't hear or we'd've all gotten suspended for fighting."

"So what's the plan for tonight? I need to blow off some steam."

Lance turned to Chris and shook his head. "Huh-uh. Don't think you're getting off that easy. Something else is going on there. I've never seen you get all defensive like that about a chick before. You don't do attachments, and that looked like some attached shit going on." Lance had crossed his arms and tipped his head back to stare Chris down.

Matt watched him, too. That same watchful expression on his face that he'd been wearing since Megan had moved in with them. Fuck.

Chris rubbed a hand over the back of his neck. "There's nothing going on. She's our roommate. I don't want assholes using her and tossing her aside. That's all."

"Since when have you ever cared if a girl gets used and tossed aside? Isn't that your standard MO?" It was Matt's turn.

"What's your problem? You've already warned me off her and I'm leaving her alone." Chris looked Matt up and down, his expression calculating. "Unless there's something you'd like to share with the group?"

Lance raised his eyebrows and turned toward Matt now. "Yes. That's a good question. Megan said she's tutoring you?"

Matt laughed at both of them. "Yeah, she's tutoring me. We have some classes together and she's really smart. She hides behind her party girl reputation, but she works hard in school."

"Uh-huh. And?" Lance gestured with one hand for Matt to go on. Chris watched with a smug smile.

"And what? She's smart and funny and she plays video games with me now that all Chris does when he's home is grunt at us and hide in his room." He shrugged. "We hang out some outside of the tutoring, but that's it."

"She plays video games?"

Matt laughed at the look of longing on Lance's face. "Yeah. She sucks, but it's more fun than playing the computer. She's super competitive and gets mad when she fucks up. It's cute. Can't get Abby to play, huh?"

"No." Lance almost looked like he was pouting. Chris couldn't help laughing. Which brought the attention back to him. Shit.

"So, now you know what the story is with Megan and me. Now it's your turn to share with the group, Chris." Matt made a sweeping gesture with his arm.

"My name's Chris and my friends are assholes."

Lance and Matt both laughed, but didn't stop looking at him, obviously expecting more than that.

He sighed. "There's nothing going on. She's our roommate. I'm not going to stand by and let some little asshole sophomore run his mouth about her." He looked at Matt. "You wouldn't either, so why is it a big deal when I do something about it?"

"Because Matt will actually date a chick that he likes. He doesn't just fuck 'em and drop 'em like you do."

"You're one to talk. Didn't you do the exact same thing?"

Lance flashed him a cocky grin. "I always took them out to dinner first, at least."

"It's not my problem that you felt the need to pay for it before you got pussy-whipped."

"Jealous?"

Chris snorted. "Not hardly."

Lance gave him a speculative look again. "I seem to remember you trying to get into Megan's pants this summer. What happened? She turn you down?"

"No."

Lance's eyebrows climbed further up his forehead. "You fucked her? And you still had the balls to ask her to move in with you guys?"

"First of all, it was Matt's brilliant idea to ask her to move in. And no, I didn't fuck her."

"But you want to." Lance made it a statement, not a question.

Chris shrugged. "She's hot. I wouldn't mind a piece of that, but Matt keeps warning me off like a jealous boyfriend."

"I told you, man. She reminds me of my little sister. I just don't want you to fuck up our roommate situation. Do you want to have to find someone mid-semester?" Matt finally jumped in.

Lance was still eyeing Chris. "I think you like her, and you want more than a one-time fuck."

"What? And get pussy-whipped like you?" Chris snorted again.

Lance just shrugged, unaffected by Chris's derision. "With the right pussy it's not a bad thing at all." A grin split his face. "Try it sometime. You might like it."

Matt broke in again. "Don't encourage him, Lance. His hands-off approach has been working so far."

Lance looked back and forth between them, his expression amused, and didn't say anything. "Alright, let's get to Chris's question. What do you guys want to do tonight? I'm out of the loop, so if there are any parties going on, it's up to you to tell me."

"Abby doesn't keep you filled in on that kind of thing?" Matt grinned too. Finally. Chris was glad the attention had moved away from him and whatever they thought might be going on with Megan. There was nothing going on. He didn't want anything going on. Yeah, sure, he'd wanted her when he'd met her over the summer, but she hadn't taken the bait like he was used to. He'd come to the conclusion that she wasn't the same type of party girl he normally used. She liked to drink and have fun, but she didn't go to parties just to hook up. That's why he'd been pissed when that little sophomore had talked about her like that. He knew she wasn't like that, and she was his roommate, so it was his job to look out for her now. Right? Right.

But he hadn't gotten laid in over a month now. With practice and away games, he'd either been too tired or not home for the parties that he'd heard about. He wondered for a moment if Megan had gone to any of those parties. It was probably best that he didn't know and hadn't been around for them. He didn't want to watch her getting groped by random guys again.

At least this time Lance and Matt would both be along with them. And Abby. They could all keep an eye on Megan while he found a jersey chaser to take the edge off.

Megan could hear the guys talking and laughing with each other as they came around the corner. Their voices trailed off as she and Abby approached and she got the feeling the guys had been talking about her. Or Abby. Maybe both of them.

Abby went straight to Lance and he wrapped his arms around her while they kissed.

Chris made coughing noises into his hand and said, "Whipped."

Without breaking away from Abby, Lance lifted one hand and flipped him off. Megan smirked. Matt came over and bumped her shoulder. "We're heading to a party. Want to ride with me? I'll be the DD, even."

She bumped him back. "I can drive. You and Chris deserve to let loose tonight."

"You sure?" His eyes searched her face.

Abby's voice broke in. "Or I can drive. We all know that I drink way less than all of you. I don't mind being the DD."

Chris shook his head. "I don't want to cram into the back seat of your tiny car, Abby. I'll drive myself. I don't feel like getting drunk tonight anyway. Matt and Megan, you guys can ride with whoever you want."

Megan watched Chris's eyes flick over her body, resting on the point where her arm was still in contact with Matt. He looked back at her face, then turned and headed toward the parking lot without waiting for anyone's answer.

She looked at Matt, who had a bemused expression on his face as he watched Chris walk away. Matt turned back to the group and slung an arm around Megan's shoulders. "I don't mind your tiny car, Abby. We can ride with you."

"Uh, thanks? We came in Lance's car, though."

Matt laughed. "Even better."

The parking lot was mostly empty by the time they got out to Lance's beat up GTO. Matt punched Lance in the shoulder. "Are you ever going to paint this old rust bucket? No wonder your dad didn't want you taking over the shop driving around in this thing."

Lance just leaned over the car and patted it on the roof. "Don't listen to him. You're beautiful."

Megan grinned and went around to the passenger side where Abby held the front seat forward so she could slide in the back, Matt getting in beside her.

The party was well underway by the time they arrived—music blaring and Marycliff students spilling out onto the front lawn. When they walked through the front door, a cheer went up from the guys on the couches at the sight of Lance and Matt. Both guys went straight over to greet their fan club.

Megan hooked her arm through Abby's. "C'mon. Let's go find the drinks." They made their way through the crowd into the kitchen. There was only beer. Megan filled a cup for each of them and handed one to Abby.

Abby wrinkled her nose in distaste. She took a sip and her expression turned into a grimace.

Megan sipped her own beer. Abby was right. It was crappy beer. She sighed, bummed that they didn't have something better to drink than this.

"How long do you think we're going to stay?"

Megan raised her eyes to Abby, who eyed her cup with disgust written on her face. Megan laughed a little. "I don't know. With beer this crappy, I wouldn't plan on staying long. But the guys getting greeted by cheers as soon as they walk through the door? They might want to stay a while."

Abby took another tentative sip and grimaced again. "Nope. It's too nasty. I can't do it. Lance keeps good beer in the house, and sometimes I'll have one of those, but even that's a stretch. I just don't like beer that much."

"Well, you're the DD anyway, so it's not like you need to drink." She took another sip. If she was in the mood to get trashed she'd chug it anyway, but she didn't feel like it tonight. "Come on. The music's good at least. Let's go see where the dancing is happening."

Megan stood on tiptoe to see over the crowd blocking the doorways and saw moving bodies on the outdoor patio. She grabbed Abby's hand so they wouldn't get separated and slipped into the stream of people moving that direction. The early September evening chilled her bare arms, but it felt good after being inside. Once they started dancing, it would be the perfect temperature.

Megan turned to face Abby and started moving to the music. It had a strong bass beat, so it was easy to dance to. Abby stood across from her, moving a little, mostly stiff. Megan laughed. "Loosen up! We're supposed to be dancing and having fun!"

Abby blushed and smiled. "I don't dance much! I feel like a complete idiot! And this is weird. Why haven't you ditched me already?"

"I don't want to get drunk bad enough to drink nasty beer. I always took you to parties with good drinks. It's not my fault you didn't want to keep up before!"

Abby laughed back at her, their shouted conversation starting to loosen her up without her realizing it. Megan smiled to herself, happy that Abby seemed to be loosening up more in general. The Abby she used to live with would never have followed her out and even tried dancing at a party. She never meant to ditch her, but Abby used to always get to a party and freeze up, hugging the wall, trying to stay out of everyone's way. Since Lance came into her life Abby followed along to get a drink, tried the beer (more than once!), and came out to the dance floor. The music was too loud to explain all that to her, though. So Megan just smiled and kept dancing, enjoying hanging out with her friend again. Enjoying being out and young and feeling the music pulsing through her body.

A hand on her hip let her know there was someone behind her, moving with her. She turned her head to see a pair of sapphire blue eyes looking down at her, fringed by dark lashes. His short dark hair was artfully mussed. He smiled and leaned close to her ear. "Mind if I join you?"

She shook her head.

He put his other hand on her hip to bracket her body. Megan turned to see Abby freezing up with another guy behind her. He was tall and good looking with medium brown hair and brown eyes. She could see Abby shaking her head at the guy, but couldn't hear her over the music.

Abby stepped closer to Megan to speak into her ear. "I'm going to go find Lance. Have fun dancing!"

As she walked away, the guy behind her leaned close to her ear again. "Your friend doesn't like to dance?"

She looked at him over her shoulder. "Not with strange guys. Her boyfriend probably wouldn't like it either."

His eyes widened a little. "What about your boyfriend?"

She grinned. "I don't have one."

He grinned back and pulled her closer to him.

Chapter Seven

"I am not drunk enough to deal with this," Chris muttered to himself. He stood near the edge of the patio and watched Megan dance with some random guy. He turned away and took another swig of his beer. His mouth twisted in distaste. Whoever got the keg did a bad job and got the cheapest thing available. They didn't even spring for liquor to make mixed drinks. Shitty party.

He'd scored the touchdown that allowed their team to win. Him, the cornerback. He'd seen the CCC quarterback about to lob a short pass, and ran full out to snatch it out of the air. He still couldn't believed they'd run a passing play of any sort so close to the end of the game with a small lead. Their stupidity was his gain. Teammates and other students passed by him and slapped him on the shoulder, offering their congratulations. He should be having fun. Celebrating. Finding a chick and taking the edge off.

Instead he was brooding in the corner watching his roommate get groped under the guise of dancing. And she didn't seem to mind. The song ended, and the sound of her laughter in the relative quiet between songs pulled Chris's attention back to her. He saw the guy in front of her now, crowding into her space, backing her toward the door to the house. Her hands went to his chest and she shook her head. Chris stood up straighter, fists clenched at his sides. No one was going to force Megan into something she didn't want. Not while he was watching. He already wanted to rip the dickhead's arms off for touching her anyway. Not that he had any right to feel that way. He had no claim on Megan. Seeing some other guy with his hands all over her pissed him off for reasons he couldn't explain, not even to himself.

The music started again, and Megan started dancing, moving away from the asshole who'd been trying to get her inside the house. Chris watched while the guy stared after her for a moment and then joined her again. He continued watching while they danced. He raised his cup to his lips again, but the bitter smell of the beer stopped him before he took another drink. He dumped out his cup in the dirt near where he stood, and leaned back to watch some more. He felt like a stalker, but he couldn't help himself. People came and went, occasionally blocking his view, but he could keep tabs on Megan and her dance partner pretty easily.

After watching that guy run his hands over Megan's ass for what had to be the hundredth time, Chris had had enough. He pushed his way past some people who picked that moment to step in front of him. The guy was behind her now, grinding his dick against Megan's ass. Chris let his hand land heavily on the guy's shoulder and pulled him away. Not too hard, but with enough strength to let the guy know he was serious and not to be fucked with.

The guy stumbled back, eyes blazing. "What the fuck, man? Find your own chick. We're dancing."

Megan had stopped dancing and turned to watch them. Chris bared his teeth in what might have passed for a smile. "Not anymore, dude. She's here with me."

He reached for Megan and pulled her against his side. He didn't look down at her, keeping his eyes on his rival, but he could feel her pushing against him, trying to get out from under his arm. He waited until the guy moved away, muttering to himself and shaking his head.

Megan landed a surprisingly hard punch to his back, just missing his kidney. He let her go, looking down at her. Her brown eyes were murderous. "What the fuck, Chris? What is your problem?"

"That asshole's my problem!" They were both yelling, as much from anger and frustration as the need to be heard. People around them stopped and moved away, not wanting to get caught in the crossfire of a budding fight.

Megan narrowed her eyes at him and tried to punch him again. He caught her wrist before she could make contact. "Watch it. I don't like being hit."

She twisted her arm in his grip, catching him off guard and going against his thumb so that he was forced to release her. "And I don't like assholes interrupting me when I'm trying to have a good time!" She turned and stormed back inside.

Chris didn't let her get far before he was after her. With the press of people going in and out of the door, it wasn't hard to catch up. He followed close behind her until his front almost touched her back. She cast a glare over her shoulder, but didn't say anything. She pushed through the crowd, headed for the living room.

Lance sat on the couch with Abby in his lap, talking to some of their mutual friends. Lance looked up when Abby started to get off his lap. Before Abby and Megan could get to each other, Chris swooped in and pulled Megan toward the front door. Lance watched all this, and he stopped Abby with a hand on her leg, tugging on her hand to convince her to sit back down. Chris lifted his chin in Lance's direction in thanks. Abby didn't look like she was going to give in, but he saw Lance say something and she relaxed back into him.

Too bad Megan didn't give in as easily. She struggled against his grip, but since he had her by the upper arm, she couldn't do that twist thing to get away again. He dragged her out through the front door, away from the bulk of the crowd so they could speak without shouting (not that he thought that was going to happen) and they'd be less likely to be interrupted. When he was satisfied with their location, he dragged Megan around to face him and let her go.

That might have been a mistake, since she immediately stepped in to hit him again. They were open palm slaps against his chest, more to vent than to try to hurt. At least he hoped so. From the way she'd almost punched him in the kidney, he was pretty sure she'd be punching him if she wanted to try to hurt him. Which she did next. Hard. Right in the solar plexus. He bent at the waist as his breath whooshed out with a grunt.

With his head closer to her level she started shouting at him. "What the fuck is wrong with you? How dare you interrupt my dancing and then drag me out here!" She slapped him on the cheek next. That stung. "Don't you ever manhandle me like that again!"

He straightened up, rubbing his cheek. "You done?"

She tipped her head back to glare at him. Man, she was pissed. "I'm not sure. It depends on what stupid thing you do or say next. I might have to knee you in the balls."

He grunted in response and ran a hand over his face to cover the smile that was fighting to get out. If she thought he'd let her get close enough to get his balls, she'd be in for a surprise.

She stared at him, waiting. After a minute she threw her hands up in exasperation. "Are you going to answer me? Or should I hit you some more until I feel better?"

"What was the question again?"

She took a step toward him, and he readied himself to block a strike to the groin. Instead, she got right up in his space and he could smell her shampoo.

"I asked you what. The. Fuck. Your. Problem. Is." She emphasized each word with a smack to the chest.

He grabbed her wrist, tired of being used as her personal punching bag. "Enough. I took it when you hit me earlier because I deserved it, but that's enough." He crowded into her personal space even more, bringing his body flush against hers. Her head was tipped back, her eyes wide, her lips parted. He wanted to kiss her. He'd been wanting to kiss her for months now. And he wanted her more now than he'd ever wanted anyone before. "As for what my problem is, you're my problem."

At his words, the pissed off expression took over her face again. "What the hell does that mean? I haven't done anything to you!"

"Fuck, Megan. I can't stand watching you dance with all these other guys, seeing them put their hands all over you, groping you. And you seem to like it. Are you out fucking around while Matt and I are gone? Having parties at our house so you're not home alone?"

She gasped and her nostrils flared. He caught her hand before it made contact with his other cheek. She struggled against his grip, but he didn't let go.

"How dare you? You have no right to accuse me of anything! You're the biggest manwhore I know! You fuck any chick that you have your eye on and dump her the minute you're done! How dare you of all people say that to me?"

She was struggling against him, so he put her arms behind her back, wrapping his arms around her middle, keeping her pressed against him, trapping one of her legs with both of his so she couldn't make good on her threat to knee him in the balls. Her tone was laced with venom, and he almost recoiled from the bite. Except he was getting more pissed off too. He was a manwhore?

But Megan wasn't done. "And it's none of your fucking business if I'm fucking anyone. You're my roommate, and a shitty one at that. I don't need you scaring off guys who I just want to dance with."

"That asshole wanted more than just a dance."

"You think I'm too stupid to know that? Just because he wants more doesn't mean I'm going to give it up."

"What do you mean I'm a shitty roommate?"

She laughed at him. "You barely say two words at a time to Matt or me. You're rude and standoffish."

She started struggling again. With the way he held her, her breasts were pushed against his chest and they rubbed back and forth with her movements. He could feel his body start to react. "Matt told me to back off and leave you alone, so I did." He spit out the words through gritted teeth.

Megan stopped struggling and looked up at him, eyes wide. "Why would he do that?"

He thrust his now hard cock against her belly. "You really don't know the answer to that question?"

Megan's eyes grew even wider, and he couldn't be sure in the dim light, but he thought her cheeks went a little pink. Who knew Megan could be made to blush? Her tongue darted out to wet her lips, and it was all Chris could do not to groan. "Why would …? What …? I don't understand."

In answer to her inarticulate questions, Chris pulled her closer and crushed his mouth to hers. She stiffened at first, but relaxed into him, opening for him when he began questing with his tongue. Her lips were soft, and he could taste the beer from the party. He wondered how much she'd had. She didn't seem drunk.

When he pulled back, she was staring up at him, looking a little dazed. He released her, letting her step back. She brought a hand to her mouth, never taking her eyes from his. Her pupils were dilated, her eyes hooded. He felt smug that he'd managed to take her from pissed off to aroused with one kiss. Or maybe, like him, she'd already been aroused from their fighting. He reached for her free hand. "Let's get out of here."

Chapter Eight

"Where are we going?" Chris had her by the hand and Megan stumbled along after him toward the sidewalk. His legs were a lot longer than hers and he was apparently in a hurry. "Chris! Slow down!"

He stopped and turned to her. "What?" The look of determination on his face changed to something else. Disappointment? "Sorry. I thought—" He looked away, over her shoulder back toward the house, and let go of her hand. She felt cold now that he wasn't touching her at all. "Do you want to go back to the party?" His voice was flat and dull.

"What? No. That party was crappy anyway. I just didn't want to get dragged behind you. I like walking."

Relief suffused his face, followed by a sheepish grin. "Sorry."

She smiled. "It's fine. Just slow down a bit, yeah? There's no fire." He reached for her hand again, and she laced her fingers through his. They started down the sidewalk at a more reasonable pace. "Where are we going?"

He glanced down at her, the hesitation back in his expression. "Home?"

When they got to his car Megan pulled out her phone to let Abby know she didn't need a ride. The drive home went by in charged silence. Chris didn't touch her again, but kept glancing at her out of the corner of his eye. Her skin was still sensitized from his touch and she shivered at the memory of his cock jabbing into her belly. She wondered what it would feel like against her skin, in her hand, inside her. It looked like she'd get to find out soon.

She was aware of him, every movement, every gesture, every expression. His hands were clenched on the steering wheel, making the muscles in his arms bulge. He ran his hand through his hair a few times, mussing it, making it stand on end. It was short, but just long enough to grab hold of. The thought of what they could be doing while she ran her hands through his hair and held on made her squirm in her seat, warmth and wetness pooling between her legs.

As soon as he threw the car in park, both their seatbelts were off and they were up the steps. Chris made short work of unlocking the door and pushing through it, closing it behind her. He turned the deadbolt and then he was on her.

He pulled her back in front of the door and pushed her up against it. His mouth was on hers, demanding entrance and capitulation. His anger from earlier was undimmed, just channeled in a new direction. She met his demands, his anger, with her own. She was turned on but still pissed off at him. For flirting with her over the summer then turning cold. For acting like an asshole. For interrupting her dance tonight. For dragging her around and acting like he owned her. For accusing her of being a slut. Not that fucking him now would prove him wrong, but she was horny and it had been a long ass time. She'd wanted Chris for a while, and she was tired of pretending otherwise. He obviously felt the same way.

His hands gripped her hips, pulling her against him, grinding her against his cock. He palmed her ass and lifted, never breaking the kiss. She wrapped her legs around him, her arms going around his neck, clasping together and hanging on.

Chris held her there, supporting her weight with his hands, and rocked against her center. Megan groaned into his mouth.

With that, he pulled her away from the door and carried her into his bedroom, his mouth still on hers, navigating by memory. It's a good thing they didn't let the house get too messy. He lowered her onto his bed, only breaking away once she lay sprawled on the mattress. He stood up and looked down at her with hooded eyes. "You look so fucking sexy sprawled on my bed with your hair a mess." He crawled on top of her again before she could respond. His hands traveled up her sides under her shirt and reached around her back to undo her bra.

Megan pushed on his chest and he sat up, letting her up too. She yanked her shirt over her head and tossed it along with her bra off to the side. That look on his face when he saw her topless was her favorite thing. His hazel eyes were darkened with desire. She'd put that look there. It made her feel wanton, sexy, powerful.

She lay back, arms up by her head, open to his gaze. He leaned forward and let his hands travel over her skin again, this time with nothing in the way. His hands were warm and rough, and she gasped when his callused fingers tweaked her nipples. He smiled down at her, his eyes meeting hers, and did it again.

Then his mouth was there. His tongue traced circles around each nipple before drawing them into his mouth one at a time. She arched into him, her fingers now in his hair like she'd imagined in the car. Deciding she'd had enough attention paid to her breasts, she tugged on his hair and brought his mouth back to hers. His t-shirt felt rough where it brushed across her oversensitive nipples. She began to pull up his shirt so she could run her hands over his torso, starting at the sides and roaming around over his back. His skin was smooth and she relished the feeling of his muscles bunching, his shoulders tight from holding himself over her.

He sat up and yanked his shirt off, throwing it like she had, and was immediately on her again. Their tongues dueled and she pressed herself against him, enjoying the feeling of his skin rubbing against hers.

He reached his hand down between them and undid her jeans then sat up and shucked them off her in one motion. He stood, removing his shoes and his shorts and boxers before he reached for a condom from his bedside table.

Megan took a moment to admire him. His chest and arms were well defined and his stomach was flat. A happy trail led from his belly button down to where he was rolling on a condom. Mmm. He was a nice size. Unless he was just a lousy lay, this should be good.

Fully covered, Chris looked up at her, his eyes sweeping down her body and back up to her face. He knelt on the bed between her legs and ran a hand up her inner thigh, spreading her legs open so he could access what he wanted. He brushed a hand over her pussy, letting his fingers trail across her mound. He did it again, more firmly. The next time, he spread her open and let a finger trace across her opening, around her clit, and back down again before slipping inside her. He pressed up, making her rock her hips, pressing herself into his hand, enjoying the feeling of his finger hitting whatever spot he'd found deep inside her. He pressed his thumb into her clit and let another finger join the first, getting her wetter.

She'd already been soaking her panties before he'd stripped them off of her. Was he going to give her an orgasm with his hand? She hoped he did and hoped he didn't at the same time. She liked the way it felt better when she came on a cock. Though his fingers did feel pretty amazing. All the heat in her body felt like it was focused between her legs where he stroked her. She clutched at the sheets, her body tightening, her hips rocking into his hand, her back starting to arch. And he pulled away, leaving her whimpering and needy.

He locked eyes with her and grinned, then slid his hands under her ass, pulling her toward him, and plunged home. Megan's eyes almost rolled back in her head. It had been months since she'd had sex, and the feeling of him filling her up was exquisite.

"Holy fuck, you're tight." Chris moved back and surged into her again. He started out slow, each thrust hard and deep, but leaving space between them. The angle he'd found was perfect and Megan couldn't help but groan each time he hit that spot, her arousal rocketing higher with each thrust. Soon, he picked up the pace. One hand left her ass and settled over her mound, his thumb sliding down to stroke her clit.

"Oh fuck oh fuck oh fuck." The words spilled out of Megan like a chant. Her body tightened, her back arching, and she exploded, all her tension unraveling as the pleasure took over.

Chris leaned forward, planting his arms on either side of her head, and picked up the pace even more, prolonging her orgasm and chasing his own. Soon he thrust hard again, and again, and he held himself against her. She was still experiencing the aftershocks of her own orgasm while he shuddered above her, his eyes tightly closed. He let out a groan and collapsed against her. He lay there for a moment, his arm and half his torso on top of hers, his cock still inside her.

His weight on her felt nice, firm and warm on top of her. Too bad it wouldn't happen again.

After a moment he got up and left the room without a word, leaving the door ajar. Megan sat up, starting to look around for her clothes. She spotted her jeans and panties first and climbed off the bed to get them so she could get dressed again. She heard the water running in the bathroom. Hers was the only room with an en suite. The guys shared the other bathroom.

The door opened and Chris came back in the room. Megan glanced up at him. He stood there naked and unselfconscious, his cock still half hard. She dropped her gaze, focused again on untangling her panties from her jeans so she could put them back on.

"What are you doing?" Chris still stood in the doorway, his arms crossed and a frown on his face.

She got her panties on and stood up, crossing her arms too. He might be unselfconscious about his nudity, but she felt at a distinct disadvantage standing in his room wearing only her panties. "Getting dressed." She kept her voice neutral, but this was a strange conversation. She hadn't pegged Chris as the type to want a cuddle and some pillow talk after sex.

He ran a hand through his hair, making it stick up some more. "I see that, but why?"

Megan's mouth hung open for a moment before she recovered herself. "Well, we, uh, finished already. I thought ..."

He lifted an eyebrow as she trailed off. He stepped all the way into the room and pushed the door closed behind him. "You thought I was done?"

Megan made a feeble gesture with one hand. "Aren't you?"

Chris stalked toward her, pulled her close, and wrapped his arms around her. "Not even close." He kissed her, his tongue sliding against hers, and pulled her back onto the bed with him. They made out for a while until Chris was ready to go again. This time was slower and they both lasted longer, their initial lust having been satisfied once already.

Once again, Chris disposed of the condom in the bathroom and came back, pulling Megan onto the bed. He turned off the light and pulled her against him, back to front so they were spooning, his arm heavy around her middle.

Megan lay wakeful in Chris's arms, trying to parse through what this meant. They'd had sex. Twice. It had been really good both times. He'd surprised her by pulling her back into his bed after both rounds.

First, she'd never done it twice in one night before, not even with a steady boyfriend. Second, she'd always heard that Chris was a wham-bam-thank-you-ma'am kind of guy. A quick fuck and you're done. Why had he pulled her back into bed, especially the second time? She'd been prepared to leave, though she hadn't started getting dressed again. But she hated the awkward conversation with a one-night stand where one person wants the other to leave. She always expected to leave afterward unless the guy asked her to hang around a while.

She'd never had a one-night stand fall asleep with her before. While she wasn't wildly experienced, she was no virgin, so this was unexpected. Chris's breathing slowed, and she felt him relax against her.

The front door had opened and closed a while ago, indicating that Matt was home. She wanted desperately to get back to her room, but didn't want to talk to Matt on the way. Especially since she hadn't even talked to Chris yet. Talking hadn't been much of a priority since they'd gotten home.

So she was stuck, cuddled up with her sleeping roommate (fuck buddy?) in his bed. She was under no illusions that this meant anything more to Chris than what it appeared. The sleeping thing was what threw her off. Did he expect her to stay here all night?

How the hell was she supposed to get back to her room?

Megan woke up groggy and puffy eyed. From the angle of the light in her room, she knew it couldn't be that late. She grabbed her phone to check the time. It wasn't even ten, why was she awake? It had been after two in the morning before she finally heard Matt go into his bedroom. She'd waited another half an hour before she'd slipped out of Chris's bed, gathered her clothes, and crept across the house to her own room.

Muffled voices let her know that the guys were awake, and that was probably what had woken her up. She stretched and got out of bed, aware of the soreness between her thighs from the two rounds last night. With a satisfied smile, she went to take a shower.

She was glad her dry spell was over, even if it wasn't under the most ideal circumstances. Not that she hadn't wanted Chris, she'd had a little crush on him since they met over the summer, but the roommate situation complicated things. Plus, Chris wasn't known for monogamy. Or dating. Or relationships of any kind. She wondered how the rest of the morning was going to play out.

Not that Megan had much room to criticize. Maybe Chris's reputation was as unearned as her own.

Everyone thought she'd slept with Isaac, but she hadn't. She knew he'd been interested, but she didn't appreciate the way he'd approached her. She'd had the occasional one-night stand, but didn't make it a habit.

When she didn't fuck him at the party where Lance and Abby had met, he'd started to view her as a challenge. He'd take her out to parties and always tried to feel her up or get her drunk enough to not be able to refuse. It hadn't worked. And he'd gotten mad, started calling her a slut and worse. And he'd spread rumors about her to his friends. Said he'd nailed her, that she was constantly calling him and begging for it, rather than the other way around.

After that she hadn't partied as much for the rest of the summer. She'd gone out with Chris and Matt when they'd invited her and stuck close to them. She knew they wouldn't let Isaac or his asshole friends get close enough to harass her. Just their presence near her was enough to scare off that kind of attention.

The downside of last night was today. Now they'd have to do the awkward morning after thing. Megan made it a point to never stay the night with a one-night stand. Not because the so-called walk of shame bothered her. No, it was the awkwardness with the other person the next day. With Chris it was unavoidable. Though, he'd done a pretty good job of avoiding her for the last few weeks. Maybe that would continue. Still, she should come up with a place to go just in case he didn't plan on making himself scarce.

After she dried off and pulled on some clothes, she decided to get breakfast. Might as well go out there and see what waited. Delaying wouldn't make anything any better.

The house was quiet when she opened her bedroom door. She stepped out and looked around. No sign of either Matt or Chris. She knew they had to be awake from the sounds she'd heard earlier. As she pulled out a bowl and her cereal she wondered what Matt would make of her sleeping with Chris. The thought of not telling him flitted through her mind, but she dismissed that as an unlikely scenario. Matt wasn't stupid, and she doubted Chris made a habit of keeping his conquests a secret. She wrinkled her nose in distaste at the thought of being categorized as a conquest, but she didn't expect anything more from him.

Speak of the devil, he walked into the kitchen wearing a pair of athletic shorts. He stopped when he saw Megan at the table, his face blank. She swallowed her mouthful of cereal as he took the last few steps toward her. He put one hand on the back of her chair, and the other on the table, leaned down and kissed her, pressing his lips to hers, but taking it no further. She almost didn't kiss him back, holding herself stiff and unmoving, but gave in after a second. His lips felt too good against hers. When he pulled back he didn't say anything, just went into the kitchen to get himself some food.

Well. Of all the reactions she'd predicted this morning, that was not on the list.

She turned to watch him, and the silence stretched out between them. He busied himself making toast and two eggs over easy. Megan turned back to her cereal, eating slowly, trying to figure out what to make of what was happening. He kissed her and wasn't talking. It brought a whole new meaning to "don't kiss and tell."

When his breakfast was ready he came and sat next to her at the table. Megan decided to wait him out and see if he would talk at all. Ha. Maybe she would avoid an awkward morning after conversation after all. He'd perfected the art of not talking to her while being in the same room already. Would he keep it up?

That kiss, though. That was different. She finished her bowl of cereal, drinking the milk straight from the bowl like she always did.

Chris swallowed his mouthful of food and finally looked at her when she set her bowl down. "Any plans today?"

Megan stared at him for a second. "Seriously?"

"What?"

Megan watched him eat his breakfast, and she wasn't sure whether to answer his question or just smack him upside the head and walk away. "You're going to just walk in and kiss me, not say anything, and then ask if I have plans?"

Chris stopped chewing to look at her, then finished his mouthful and swallowed. "Yeah. Is that a problem?"

"I don't even know how to answer that question." She got up from the table and took her bowl to the sink.

When she looked at him again, he was sitting back in his chair, his gaze sweeping over her body. "It's a pretty straightforward question."

"You want to know if I have plans today." He nodded. She leaned against the counter and crossed her arms. "Why?"

"To see if you want to hang out or do something together." He gave her a look like she wasn't too quick on the uptake.

She narrowed her eyes at him. "You want to hang out with me. Since when?"

He got up and brought his now-empty plate to the sink. He set it down, and his eyes never left hers. He stepped into her personal space, crowding her, causing her to take a step to the side, and another, until he'd backed her into the corner. He placed his arms on either side of her, bracketing her in, bringing his face closer to level with hers. Megan was acutely aware of the fact that he wasn't wearing a shirt. This close she could smell him, a combination of him, hints of his spicy cologne, and sex from the night before. He hadn't showered and washed her off. That fact alone made her clench her thighs against the burst of arousal she felt there.

He dipped his head, capturing her gaze, his hazel eyes blazing with intensity. "Since July."

Her brows came together. "Since July? Really?"

He nodded and flashed a grin. "You were hung up on that other guy that pissed you off right before the party on the Fourth, and weren't very receptive to my advances. After that you didn't seem interested in anyone, so I didn't pursue anything."

"You have a reputation."

There was that cheeky grin again. "I do."

"I wasn't interested in a one-time fuck."

A shrug. "I gathered."

"But now you've had me, so … what is this?"

He dipped his head closer so he could whisper in her ear. "Once with you is not nearly enough."

Megan fought to keep from squirming at his words and the tone of voice in which he delivered them. No wonder this guy had his pick of girls. With that body, that panty-dropping smile, and that voice, girls probably stripped down on the spot for him. She'd obviously not been the recipient of the full force of his charm before this. Sure, they'd flirted, but he'd never actually tried to seduce her. And now she knew why.

She put her hands on his chest to push him back so she could have some space to breathe, to think, but the push turned into something more like a caress. "So, what? You want to start dating now?"

He shrugged again and leaned into her touch a little. "If that's what you want to call it, sure."

"So this was your way of asking me out?"

Something flashed across his face. Was he embarrassed? "I guess so. Are you going to say yes?"

"I have some homework I need to get done today, but otherwise I'm free. What did you have in mind?"

Chapter Nine

Instead of answering her question, Chris took advantage of their position and kissed her. She didn't respond at first, but softened after a second, leaning into him. It was the same reaction he'd gotten when he'd kissed her at the table. Stiffness followed by relaxing into his kiss.

They were pretty tame kisses—no tongue. He was holding himself in check. Really, he wanted to devour her again, take her back to his room and spend the day with her there. Since she'd put up some resistance already, he didn't think that would be an option.

So, homework and a date. He just wanted to spend time with her, be able to touch her. He was done denying himself what he'd been craving for so long now. He hadn't been lying. One night wasn't nearly enough to work her out of his system.

It was a strange feeling, but he didn't want to fight it. His instincts on the field led him to be one of the top players on the team, so he was used to going with what he felt in the moment. Why should this be any different?

He broke the kiss and pulled back so he could look down into her upturned face. Her eyes fluttered open. They were a warm dark brown, pupils dilated, lids heavy. He smiled. "Do you have a lot of homework?"

She blinked a couple times. "What? Oh, right. Homework. I just have some reading for tomorrow."

Chris straightened up and took a small step back. Megan seemed to take a deeper breath and her eyes came into sharper focus. His smile grew a little wider. "Why don't you get started and then we'll go out for lunch later, maybe catch a movie after. Sound good?"

Her eyes remained fixed on his, but she nodded. He moved to the side, out of the way, so she could get past. She moved slowly at first, holding his gaze as she stepped away from the counter, then faster as she gained ground and moved farther away from him.

He went back to his room to take a quick shower and change clothes. He grabbed one of his textbooks to take out to the living room for the pretense of doing homework. He probably did have homework. Maybe he should find a syllabus to check and see what he needed to do for any of his classes. But that would require remembering where he'd put that stuff.

He couldn't be bothered to care since he wouldn't be coming back next semester. His hopes of going pro, or even doing something like arena football, didn't look like they were going to pan out. This was his last chance. He went to classes. Some of the time, anyway. But why bother doing homework when your GPA didn't matter anymore? When you weren't planning on graduating anyway? He only went to class as much as he did to keep the coach off his ass.

The living room was empty. What the hell? Where was Megan? Her bedroom door was closed. He went over and rapped his knuckles against the wood and waited. A minute later Megan opened the door. Her curls were everywhere like she'd just shoved her hand through her hair and not bothered to make sure they landed back in place. He smiled, reaching out a hand to touch her hair.

She dodged his hand, and he pulled his eyes back to her face. "What do you want, Chris? I thought you were going to let me do my homework first."

He held up his textbook. "I thought we could study together."

She eyed him with a wary expression. "You want to do homework together?"

"You do homework with Matt all the time." He couldn't help the defensiveness that crept into his voice.

"That's different. I'm tutoring Matt and we have classes together. I don't even know what your major is."

"Exercise Science. And anyway, we're both just reading. You don't have to help me. You read your stuff, and I'll read mine. Come sit on the couch with me."

Megan's eyes searched his face like she might be expecting him to start laughing that she'd believed a practical joke. When he didn't say anything else she finally nodded. "Okay."

Chris waited while she gathered her book, notebook, pen, and highlighters. This chick took her reading seriously. She followed him out to the couch. He sat down on one end. When she went to the other end to sit he shook his head and patted the middle cushion. "Sit here. Next to me."

She looked at him again like she was trying to figure him out. After a minute she shrugged and sat down, setting her notebook on the couch next to her.

He put his feet up on the coffee table, ankles crossed, his textbook open on his lap. Megan sat cross legged on the couch, her book open across her legs, her notebook next to her. She kept her highlighter in the gutter of the book and her pen in her hand. She chewed on the cap while she read.

Chris stretched his arm out along the back of the couch behind her. She was so intent on her reading that she didn't notice. Or at least she pretended not to. Every so often Chris would turn a page. He'd picked a chapter at random. He stared at the pages, sometimes reading the bold faced headings and the captions under the images. He'd apparently grabbed an anatomy book and was now looking through the chapter on arm and shoulder muscles.

Time passed. Megan shifted. Her left leg was still curled up under her, the right was down. Every so often she'd write something in her notebook or highlight something in the text.

Chris found himself watching her study more than he pretended to read his own book. He wanted to touch her. To run his hand over the curve of her back where she sat forward over her book. Or, better yet, pull her over so she could relax against him, his arm around her instead of along the back of the couch. It would be even better if they were watching a movie instead of studying—or pretending to, in his case.

"Enjoying yourself?" Megan's words pulled him out of his thoughts of what he'd like to happen once the hypothetical movie was over. She was still looking at her book, highlighting something.

He shifted in his seat, making room in his shorts for his semi that was well on its way to becoming more. "What?"

She turned her head to look at him and put the cap back on her highlighter with a click. "I can't help but notice that you're studying me instead of that." She nodded toward the book in his lap.

He closed the book. No point keeping up the pretense. "I don't really need to study. I was just using it as an excuse."

He had her full attention now. She'd put her pen and highlighter down and closed her book. "You don't need to study? At all?"

He shrugged. "I'm not coming back next semester, so why bother? My GPA doesn't matter anymore."

She frowned at him, her brows drawn together. "Why wouldn't you come back next semester?"

He shrugged. "What's the point?"

"Uh, so you can finish your degree."

He made a noncommittal sound in response, not wanting to talk about this. Instead, he did what he'd been wanting to do and ran his hand down her back, then up and around the nape of her neck, until coming to a stop cupping the back of her head, his fingers tangled in her curls. He sat forward and brought his mouth to hers. She kissed him back right away this time. There was none of the hesitation from earlier this morning. That seemed like a good sign. He pulled back. "Are you done studying?"

She nodded. "Yeah. You're too distracting."

He couldn't suppress a triumphant grin. "Good." He leaned down to kiss her again, and she turned into him, her hands going to his chest. He wrapped his arms around her, pulled her against him and onto his lap, and leaned back so they could be more comfortable.

After a moment Megan sat up and looked around. "Where's Matt?"

"Who cares?" He pressed up against her so she could feel what was really on his mind.

She grinned down at him. "Well, I doubt he'd want to walk in on us. Is he even here? I haven't seen him all day."

"No. I think he left this morning. No idea where he went."

The grin faded from her face and she looked a little concerned. "I heard you guys talking this morning. Did you tell him about us?"

"He'd figured it out on his own. Matt's not stupid."

Megan nodded, the furrow still between her eyebrows.

His hands went to her hips and he pushed her down, sliding her against him some more, wanting to distract her and get her focus back where he wanted it. Fuck, that felt good. Not as good as the real thing, though. "Is that a problem?"

Megan's eyes closed and she sighed. He was getting to her. Good. "I don't know. Was he okay with it?"

"He seemed fine. Do you really want to talk about Matt right now?"

She shook her head. "Not right now."

He pulled her head back down to his, tangling his tongue with hers once more. She groaned into his mouth. He loved hearing those sexy sounds from her. It was his turn to groan when she broke away again. Only his groan was frustration, not arousal.

She laid her head on his shoulder. "Chris, I'm, um, a little sore." Her voice was a whisper.

He pulled his head back a little so he could look at her face. "Sore?"

Her cheeks looked a little pink. "From last night. It's been a while, and we did it twice."

"It's been a while? But I thought—"

She cut him off. "Yeah, I can guess what you thought. Don't believe everything you hear."

He studied her face. "Okay." He pulled her in for another kiss and let his hands roam over her back and then up under her shirt. She pulled back again, and he growled.

"I'm serious, Chris. I'm not up for sex right now. My lady bits need a break."

"It's okay. I just want to make you feel good. If anything hurts, I'll stop. I promise." He ground his pelvis against her again, watching her eyelids flutter in response, and that breathy sigh escape her lips. "Does that hurt?"

"N-no."

He smiled, pure male satisfaction. "Good. But you're right. We should probably move this out of the living room."

He stood her up and started to lead her by the hand toward his bedroom, stopping when she tugged at his hand. He looked back to see why she'd stopped. She tilted her head toward her own room. "Let's use my room. I have my own bathroom."

He nodded, allowing her to lead the way now. He felt a little weird coming in here to get naked with someone. In some part of his mind this was still Lance's room, and he never would've done this while Lance still lived here.

Once inside, though, all thoughts of it being Lance's room vanished. It looked so different. There was only a twin bed, for one thing, that Megan had moved with her from her tiny apartment. The furniture was different—Lance had taken his old stuff when he'd moved in with Abby. And there were pictures on the walls—framed art prints of famous works, what looked like original paintings in some places, and framed photos of friends and family on top of her dresser.

The twin bed wasn't ideal. On the plus side, it meant they'd have to stay very close together. That wasn't such a bad thing.

Chris closed the door behind him, then drew Megan to him by their connected hands. She came willingly, no hesitation, desire making her pupils large and her eyelids heavy. He cupped her face with his free hand and placed a gentle kiss on her lips before he slid his tongue along her lower lip and deepened the kiss. She responded, pressing her body against his, her tongue seeking out his, sliding and tangling. His hand slid from her cheek to tangle in her curls and tilted her head back so he could plunder her mouth more thoroughly. Her soft moan had his cock swelling even more, pressing against her through their clothes.

He released his hold on her hair and brought his hands down her back to run over her ass before sliding under and lifting. Megan broke their kiss, her eyes widened in surprise, but she wrapped her legs around his waist and her hands clutched his shoulders. He gave her a cocky grin and carried her over to the bed where he sat with her in his lap once more.

Not wasting time, he slid his hands under her shirt and lifted it up. Megan raised her arms, perfectly understanding his intentions. He tossed the shirt somewhere, not paying attention where, his eyes now focused on her breasts. She wore a simple pink cotton bra, but it might as well have been the sexiest lingerie the way his mouth watered. He'd seen her breasts last night. He already knew how they filled his hands just right, and the way her dusky nipples peaked when he teased them with his tongue. Seeing them in the daylight that filtered through her curtains was even better than in the lamplight in his room last night. He tugged the cups out of the way so that her breasts were propped up like an offering just for him. With her on his lap, her breasts were at the perfect height. He took one nipple in his mouth immediately, sucking hard to draw it in and flick his tongue across the tip until it grew puckered and hard in his mouth. Megan's hands gripped his hair, holding him in place while she threw her head back and moaned. He pulled back, sucking on her nipple until it released with a pop, then turned his attention to the other one.

He went back and forth between her breasts for a while. He felt like he could almost stay there forever. When she was grinding her hips against him, letting out the sexiest sighs and moans he'd ever heard, he shifted, turning so he could lay her down on the bed. He kissed each nipple one last time before he drew his tongue down her torso in a line to the top of her jeans. He looked her in the eye while he unbuttoned and unzipped her jeans, tugging them down along with her panties. She lifted her hips to help him, and he stood up to strip them all the way off and toss them away like her shirt.

Concern flashed on Megan's face. "Chris, I—"

"Shh." He ran his hands over her skin, and leaned down for a kiss. "I know. I promise to just make you feel good." She nodded and kissed him again. He broke away to look down at her spread out on the bed for him, her breasts still offered up by her bra, her skin smooth and soft. He ran his hands over her breasts, tweaking her nipples, eliciting a gasp from her. Then he moved them down over her hips, on the outside of her legs, down to her knees, and slid back up between her thighs. He settled himself there, his hands spreading her legs to make room for his shoulders.

He'd been in such a hurry to get inside her last night that he hadn't taken his time to enjoy the feel of her skin like he was now. He trailed kisses up the inside of her right thigh, stopping at the crease where leg joined torso, and repeated the action on the other side.

When he stopped again, just letting his breath fan over her pussy spread before him, she squirmed and whimpered. "Chris ..." His name was a plea on her lips.

He smiled widely, even though she couldn't see it. He was driving her as crazy as she drove him. If the wetness gathering at the opening of her shiny pink lips wasn't proof enough, her other reactions were. He reached out with his tongue and licked firmly from bottom to top. He paused before he did it again, increasing the pace, then circled around her inner labia and clit with his pointed tongue. He alternated those until she was squirming against his mouth, pleading for more. Sucking her clit into his mouth and flicking it with his tongue, he stopped teasing her and gave her what she was begging for. She came moments later, bucking and shuddering with her release.

Chris crawled up her body, kissed her deeply once, and settled next to her, pulling her against him.

Megan lay still in his arms for a moment before her hand glided down the front of his shirt and up under the hem to run her hand over his bare chest. She caressed his flat stomach, then up to play with each of his nipples. He shivered under her touch.

She sat up. His skin felt chilled by the sudden removal of her warmth. She reached behind her with both hands, momentarily pressing her breasts forward, and her bra was off, her breasts still perky without it, but hanging more naturally now that they weren't squished together and up by the out of place cups.

Throwing one leg over him, she straddled him again, settling herself over where his straining cock was still imprisoned in his shorts. She reached for his shirt again and started to push it up his torso. "My turn."

Megan pushed Chris's shirt up and out of the way, leaning forward to trace one nipple with her tongue like he'd done to her the night before. She enjoyed the way he shivered and squirmed beneath her.

"Fuck, Megan. You're killing me."

She sat up again with a self-satisfied smile and pulled on his shirt some more to indicate she wanted it off. He sat up a little and yanked it over his head before he settled back against the pillow. She leaned down again, this time kissing him on the mouth, sliding her tongue inside, tasting the tang of her own juices there. She sat back up and ran her hands down his chest, over his abs, until she got to the button of his shorts. With a flick of her fingers she undid it and looked him in the eye while she scooted back just enough to undo his zipper. She reached in the opening she'd made and tugged down his boxers so she could wrap her fingers around his cock.

Chris groaned, closing his eyes, and his cock twitched in her palm. She let him go and got up. Chris's eyes flew open, but he relaxed when she started to tug down his shorts and boxers, lifting his hips to help get them off. Now it was her turn to admire him. She hadn't taken in more than the barest of details last night between the low lighting and their hurried coupling.

She'd seen him shirtless before, but it was different now that she got to touch him, and she planned to take her time looking and touching to her heart's content. His upper body was tan all over, though his arms, muscular and defined, were slightly darker than his chest. It was obvious that he'd spent a lot of time shirtless over the summer. There was a clear delineation between his torso and the skin below his waistband, the golden brown stopped short and became a paler version over his hips. His cock stood out, long and thick and firm, nestled in a thicket of darker hair. His muscular thighs were the same pale shade as his hips, and they faded to the same golden tan as his chest as they approached his knees. Mmm. Football players were hot.

Megan ran her hands up his legs, starting at his ankles. She massaged his thighs with her fingers, settling herself on the bed between them, then ran her hands up over his hips, bypassing his cock, causing him to suck in a breath when she acted like she was going to touch it again, but circled around to caress his lower stomach and ran her hands over the happy trail that ran from navel to groin. She gave him a wicked smile and he let out a pained groan.

"Touch me. Please." His voice was hoarse, his muscles tense from holding himself still while she explored his body.

She smiled her wicked smile again. "I am touching you." She tweaked a nipple to emphasize her point.

He growled and bucked his hips a little, trying to make contact with any part of her he could. "That's not what I fucking meant."

Megan's smile grew wider, but she ran her hands back down his torso and framed his cock between her thumbs and index fingers for just a moment before she slid one hand down to his balls while the other circled his cock. She pumped him slowly and he groaned, thrusting against her hand. She worked him with her hand for a moment before she leaned down and swirled her tongue around the crown. He shuddered in reaction, his balls tightening up a little in her other hand. She smiled and held him steady so she could lick from the base to the head before she swirled her tongue around again. Enjoying his reactions, she did it a few more times, keeping just far enough away that he couldn't thrust into her mouth when she reached the crown each time. And he tried.

She waited to take him all the way in her mouth, teasing him like he'd teased her. She decided to take his incoherent moans and whimpers as begging, and with one more swirl of her tongue, closed her lips over the head of his cock. Sucking and running her tongue around the underside, he bucked against her, but she was expecting it at this point, and took him further into her mouth. She kept ahold of him, now working her hand in tandem with her mouth. He was getting close. It was obvious from the way he bucked his hips and the way his balls had pulled tight against his body. All the muscles in his body were tight, his hands clutching her comforter in tight fists.

He groaned again. "I'm gonna—" She held still, allowing him to thrust into her mouth, sucking hard, until she felt him erupt. He shuddered on the bed, and she smiled again as well as she could with him still in her mouth. She loved being able to reduce a man to this, especially one as built and sexy as this one. After he finished she released him, sitting up to survey her handiwork.

His hands caught her under the armpits, and he pulled her up to lay full length on his body so he could kiss her again. He broke away and settled her against him, both of them barely fitting on her small bed. "Holy shit." His voice was still husky and strained. Megan's lips curved in a smug smile. He dropped a kiss on her head. "If your bed were bigger, I'd take a nap. Instead, we'll lay here until we're uncomfortable or one of us falls off, and then we'll go to lunch."

Chapter Ten

Chris held the restaurant door open for Megan. It was after two on a Sunday and the usual lunch crowd had cleared, so they got a table right away. He'd opted for Fire, the fancy pizza place. He didn't know what was expected for a date on a Sunday afternoon. Megan was in jeans and he wore shorts, so a really upscale place didn't seem like a good choice. He'd been here a couple of times and the food was good.

Once they'd ordered their pizza and the waitress had gone, Chris fidgeted a little, tapping his fingers on the table.

Megan studied him over the top of her glass. "Nervous?"

He stopped his hands through sheer force of will. "Nope. Why?" He managed to keep his voice casual. Good.

A grin spread across Megan's face. "You're bouncing your leg like crazy."

Shit. He stopped that too. "I don't know what you're talking about." That casual tone he'd managed before? Nope, gone now. He was such a bad liar sometimes. Megan just laughed at him and he smiled. "Fine. I don't take girls out very often."

"How often is not very often?" Megan's tone was dry, and her lips twitched with suppressed laughter. He appreciated that she was trying not to laugh in his face, even though part of him was kind of annoyed that she found it so amusing that he was flustered. He didn't get flustered with girls, dammit. But he didn't date girls either.

He screwed up his face like he was deep in thought. "Hmm. About never."

Megan lost her fight with her laughter and let it out. She didn't hold back when she laughed—no simpering giggles like so many girls used when they flirted with him.

Her laughter died down and she studied him again, the humor now gone from her face. "So, this is a date."

He nodded and took a drink of his soda, wondering where she was going with this. Hadn't they established this morning that this was a date?

"Does that mean we're dating?"

He shrugged. "What would that mean, exactly?"

"Don't worry, you don't have to take me out to eat all the time or anything." She flashed him a big grin and he smiled back. "But no fucking anyone else while we're together. If you want to end it, have the balls to end it with me before you hook up with another chick."

It was his turn to study her face. The waitress showed up then with their food. What impeccable timing. He waited for her to leave before he returned his attention to Megan. "Sounds fair. And it goes both ways."

"Of course." She maintained eye contact, her brown eyes holding his like she was trying to see inside him without giving anything away. Finally she flashed her smile again and got a slice of pizza.

Their conversation relaxed after that. She seemed satisfied with his answers about their relationship, such as it was. Relationship. That was a loaded word. Their ... shit. He couldn't come up with anything better than relationship. In any case, he was happy she didn't push for more than he was able to give. Exclusivity didn't seem like too big of a deal. Especially since he hadn't wanted anyone else since he'd met her.

Chris ran into Megan's back when she stopped in the open door to their house. He dropped his hands to her hips to steady both of them and looked over her head to see Matt sitting on the couch, a Playstation controller in his hand. His eyes flicked to them and back at the screen before he paused the game and tossed the controller on the coffee table in front of him. He grabbed an open beer from the table and sat back, taking a pull and letting his eyes wander over both of them, pausing on Chris's hands on Megan's hips.

Matt was a master at keeping his thoughts to himself, so his face didn't give anything away as he looked them over. He gestured to them with the beer as he swallowed. "So you two are a thing now?"

Megan tilted her head back to look up at Chris, her eyes large and uncertain, and he dropped a kiss on her mouth before he nudged her so she would go the rest of the way inside. Chris closed the door behind him and let his hands drop away from Megan. "Yup."

He went into the kitchen and grabbed a beer for himself, poking his head back out to hold one up to Megan, wordlessly asking if she wanted one. She still stood in the living room, arms crossed, looking from him to Matt and back again. She shook her head at him, and he popped the top off his beer and came back in the living room.

Sitting on the couch, he pulled Megan down into his lap. She sat stiffly, but he wouldn't let her push away from him. This was how things were going to be. No sense wasting time being awkward about it. Matt watched them, his face impassive.

Chris pointed with the neck of his bottle at the game frozen on the TV. "Wanna play me or finish your game against the computer?"

Matt shrugged and set his beer back down. "Sure, we can play. It's been awhile, you sure you're still any good?"

Chris grinned and got up to get the other controller, shoving Matt's shoulder while he exited the game and got a new one started. "Don't worry. I can still take you."

Matt looked across him to where Megan now sat curled into the corner of the couch. "Don't worry. You can play next game."

She just nodded, still looking like she wasn't quite sure what to make of everything. Chris sat back and kissed her again. She responded slowly, like she was shocked he'd kiss her so casually in front of Matt. He pulled back and grinned at her. "Relax. It's all good," he whispered next to her ear. A trail of goosebumps raised on her neck, and he couldn't suppress his smug smile at how he affected her. But she relaxed and settled into her usual position on the couch, with her legs curled under her. After a while she ended up with her feet in his lap, leaning against the arm of the couch, watching him and Matt blow things up on their video game.

Chris smiled to himself, feeling like he could relax in his house again. Things were going better than he could've ever expected. Hopefully it would last for longer than the weekend.

Megan woke up the next morning to a warm body pressing her into the bed and light kisses on her mouth. She cracked her eyelids open to see Chris's face hovering above hers in the dim light.

He pressed one more kiss to her lips. "Sorry, I didn't want to wake you, but I don't know what time you usually get up. I have to get to the gym before breakfast and classes and didn't want you to oversleep."

She stretched and adjusted underneath him so that he settled more firmly between her legs. She arched into him and confirmed the erection she thought she'd felt through the fabric of his boxers. They'd slept in their underwear since she still hadn't felt up for actual sex. Chris hadn't pushed it, but he had insisted that she sleep in his room.

Chris let out a little groan when she rubbed against him again. A satisfied smile crept onto her face at the sound. He ground his pelvis into hers once before he shook his head. "I'd love to, but there's not enough time. I'll take a raincheck."

She poked out her lower lip in a mock pout. He chuckled in response. "What time is it?" Her voice was still raspy with sleep. They'd stayed up late talking, and she was still really tired.

"About six forty-five. I have to be at the gym by seven thirty."

She groaned and closed her eyes again, throwing an arm over her face. Rolling over and pulling the blankets over her head wasn't an option since Chris was still on top of her. "It's so early. My first class isn't until ten." She batted at his chest. "Let me go back to sleep."

He chuckled again and kissed her once more before he got up. "Do you need me to set an alarm for you?"

"No." Her voice was muffled since she'd rolled face down into the pillow. "I have one set on my phone."

She felt his lips brush her bare shoulder and raised her head to look at him. He smiled. "See you tonight."

"Bye."

The three of them fell into a much more relaxed routine. Chris no longer felt like he needed to stay gone from the house as much as possible in order to avoid Megan. Matt had pulled him aside once and said, "Don't fuck this up, dude. She's like my little sister and I don't want to see her get hurt." Chris had just nodded and Matt had dropped the subject after that. The watchful look that he'd worn whenever Chris and Megan had been in the same room at the start of the semester was gone, and things went back to normal between them.

Chris touched Megan a lot, but mostly kept it PG when Matt was around. He did like to sneak in a grope here and there when Matt was in the room but not paying attention to make her jump and glare at him. He always liked getting her riled up. And the more riled up she got out of the bedroom, the more fun they had in the bedroom.

Midway through their first week together, they'd moved Chris's bed into Megan's room. Chris was happy to give up his old room for the master suite, and they could both fit on his queen-sized bed much better than her twin.

The other benefit of spending time with Megan was that she forced Chris to study. After that first time when he faked his way through reading while she did her homework, she made him get out all his syllabi and do some homework. That meant his coach didn't ride his ass so much about his academics.

They got to spend every evening together during their first couple of weeks as a couple. Then they had away games two weekends in a row. The first one didn't seem so bad, but the second one had Chris on edge and off his game.

He'd talked to Megan on the phone on Friday night in their hotel room. Since Matt was in the room, they didn't talk much or for long. Chris felt awkward talking to her on the phone where Matt could hear every word he said, even though he seemed cool with them being together.

To Matt's credit, he acted like nothing unusual was going on and didn't react at all to Chris's phone conversation. In some ways that made it worse. He was used to Matt giving him shit for anything and everything. That's how they did things. For him to play it off like nothing was going on was almost as bad as if they'd had some awkward conversation about it.

Saturday night after the game, he fell facedown into his bed, exhausted. He'd been pulled out at halftime because he'd let too many passes slip through. He was known as the best picker on the team. For him to not get one interception and then to get scored on almost every play he was involved in burned.

His phone buzzed with a text alert. He groaned and lifted his head, swiping his phone off the nightstand. It was Megan.

How was the game?

Shitty. He kind of hoped she'd let it go at that. But last week she'd asked the same question and pressed for more details. She understood more about football than he'd expected, given that she'd told him she didn't usually go to their games.

So you lost?

Yeah. They'd never managed to recover from the touchdowns his defense had let slip through in the first half. They'd held them in the second half, but couldn't bring up their own score.

Do you want to call me and talk?

He thought about that one for a moment. He didn't want to talk at all. Would she get pissed if he said that? *Not really. Matt's watching a movie. I don't want to bother him.* There. That seemed like a good reason not to talk. It wasn't that he didn't want to talk to her. Just not on the phone. If he were honest, even if he were home, he wouldn't want to talk. He played a shitty game. He wanted to feel better, not rehash it more than he'd already have to with the coaching staff.

Okay.

Good. She wasn't pissed. Or at least she wasn't telling him if she was, and he was pretty sure Megan wouldn't hold back on that.

I bet I know something that will make you feel better.

Now he was intrigued. A minute later he got another text. There were no words, just a picture of her breasts, looking down at her cleavage. She didn't have a shirt on, just a lacy red bra. He let out an audible groan.

"You alright, man?" Matt glanced over from where he sat on his own bed, a look of concern on his face.

"Yeah. Fine. Just tired." Shit. Now he was going to have to deal with having a hard-on while he shared a room with another guy. "I'm gonna go take a shower."

"Again?"

"Yeah." Thank God his bed was the one closer to the bathroom. It meant he didn't have to walk past Matt with his cock leading the way.

He turned on the shower and spent the next ten minutes sexting with Megan, detailing what he'd like to do to her, and reading what she'd like to do to him. His cock got harder the longer it went on. He sat on the edge of the tub stroking himself with one hand, looking at the sexy pics Megan sent and texting her back with the other. When he couldn't take it anymore, he set his phone down and climbed in the shower all the way, stroking himself harder and faster, imagining it was Megan getting him off. When he came, he came hard. It was the best orgasm he'd ever had by himself. He turned off the shower and picked up his phone again while toweling off.

Holy fuck that was hot.

All he got in response was a winking smiley and a lips emoji. He smiled to himself and sent one more text.

I've gotta go to bed now. See you tomorrow.
Goodnight.

Chapter Eleven

Megan stood and cheered as Marycliff University scored a touchdown, putting them in the lead by five points with only seconds left on the clock. Abby stood next to her bouncing on her toes, and Lance was on her other side yelling as loud as anyone. The whole section of students and alumni shouted "Moooo!" and held up their hands to form the letters M and U in sign language. After the extra point, the opposing team started a play, but it was a half-hearted effort at best. Their pass was blocked, ending the game.

Megan, Abby, and Lance waited while the crowd around them cleared out, packing up the extra sweatshirts and blankets they'd brought to stay warm in the chilly October evening. Since they'd have to wait for Chris and Matt before they headed to an afterparty, they weren't in any hurry to get out and it was easier to wait for the crowds to disperse.

"So things have changed a bit since the last time we were at a game." Abby folded her blanket and pushed it into her tote bag, glancing at Megan out of the corner of her eye.

Megan paused, watching Abby for a moment before she answered. "Yup."

"That's all you're going to give me?" Abby had stopped getting her things together and just stared at Megan.

Megan's gaze flicked to Lance, who seemed to be fighting back a smile while he pretended to ignore their conversation altogether. She shrugged. "There's not that much to tell. What do you want to know?"

Abby's mouth dropped open in shock. "Megan, you were always oversharing with me when we lived together. I can't believe you haven't called me and given me more details than I ever wanted to know. All I know is that you and Chris are together now. How's it going? Is it weird living with the guy you're dating right from the beginning of the relationship?"

Megan leveled a look at Abby. "You'd know as much about that as I would. You practically moved in with Lance after like a week."

"Not the same thing at all." Abby shook her head and narrowed her eyes. "We didn't live together *before* we started dating. And I still had our apartment to escape to if I ever needed it. You don't."

Megan just shrugged and let a smirk take over her face. "I can't believe you're pumping me for details about my relationship. Are you wanting to compare notes on the sex?"

Lance let out a bark of laughter, causing them both to look at him. He covered it with a fake coughing fit and turned away from them.

Abby faced Megan again, her eyes narrowing. "You know I wouldn't do that. And especially not in a public place."

"Well, you never know. You've changed since you started dating Lance." Megan feigned nonchalance and continued to put her things in her own bag, fighting back a smile while Abby spluttered.

"I have not!"

Megan couldn't hold back her smile anymore and she let out a chuckle to go with it. "Yes you have,

Abby. It's not a bad thing. You're still our lovable Abby, you're just a little more … loose."

"I'm *loose*?!"

Megan was cracking up by now and so was Lance, though he was still trying to hold it in. His shoulders shook and she thought she saw him wiping tears from his eyes. Megan shook her head. "Not like that, Abby. I just mean you've loosened up."

Abby glared at her for a moment longer, firmly seating her bag on her shoulder. "Whatever. That's completely beside the point. We're not talking about Lance and me. We're talking about you and Chris."

Megan sighed a little. "I told you already, there's not much to tell. We're together, or dating, or whatever you want to call it."

"Is it getting serious?" Abby leaned in and lowered her voice a little.

"It's only been a few weeks, Abby. And it's Chris. How serious could it be?" When she looked away from Abby, she caught Lance's face again. The laughter was gone, and he examined her. Their eyes met for a moment and he raised a brow at her. She let out another breath and looked away from him too, focused on zipping her bag closed.

"Fine. We sleep in the same room when he's not away for games because it's easier than one of us having to get up in the middle of the night, get dressed again, and go to the other side of the house. And Matt doesn't have to see or hear anything he doesn't want to."

Lance snorted again.

"Eww." That was Abby.

Megan rolled her eyes. "Please. It's not like you're not loud. I walked in on you guys that one time, remember? And I know what happened in your room afterward."

Pink spread across Abby's cheeks. Megan chuckled again. "You brought it up. If you don't want details, you shouldn't ask."

Abby lifted her nose and set her mouth in a prim line. "I only asked because I care about you. I want you to be happy."

Megan softened a little and decided to stop giving Abby a hard time. "Thanks. I appreciate it. I am happy. I just know how things are and have appropriate expectations." She shrugged again and bumped Abby's shoulder with hers as they turned to make their way down the steps to leave the stadium. "We can't all have what you have so quickly and easily."

Abby didn't say anything after that. Lance reached back and laced his fingers with hers, his obvious love and affection for the little blonde written all over his face. Megan held in a wistful sigh. Despite what she'd told Abby, she was starting to develop stronger feelings for Chris than she let on. She couldn't bring herself to admit it out loud. She could barely admit it to herself. There was no way she was going to talk about that with Abby, especially with Lance standing there watching and listening. The last thing she needed was for Chris to suspect that he meant more to her than just the casual relationship they had going.

Their relationship was born of attraction and proximity. Chris's track record with women didn't inspire thoughts of rings and wedding bells. Or even anything approaching a significant commitment. She knew there would be an end date. And she hoped like hell that she could keep her heart out of it as much as possible until that day came.

"Hey." Chris smiled and pulled Megan in for a kiss. "Did you drive?"

"No. I rode with Abby and Lance."

"Good." He pulled her tighter against him and kissed her again, this time longer than before. He could feel her hands clutching at his sweatshirt, pulling him closer.

A throat cleared behind her, and she pushed Chris away. He grinned down at her, keeping one arm wrapped around her before turning to face Lance, who had a look of cocky amusement on his face and his arms wrapped around Abby in front of him. He lifted his chin from where it rested on her head. "You done?"

Chris tilted his head to the side, feigning contemplation. "For now."

Lance laughed. "Right." His eyes flicked over Chris's shoulder. "Matt, you wanna drive or ride with Abby and me?"

Matt's eyes moved back and forth between the two couples, his hands in his pockets and his shoulders hunched. "If Abby's going to drive us home again, I'll ride with you guys. I think I need a drink or five if I'm going to be the third wheel."

Chris couldn't help snickering, but stopped when Megan stepped away from him to loop her arm through Matt's. "You're not a third wheel. But I think I'll join you in the drinking." She cast a glance back at Chris over her shoulder and grinned. "Chris is driving tonight, so I don't need to stay sober either."

Matt looked down at her, laughing, the affection clear on his face. Chris ground his teeth and fought back a surge of jealousy. He knew that she and Matt were friends, and they hung out together when he wasn't around. But he wanted her to drink with him, even if his drinking was restricted for the night. They'd won the game, he'd played well, and he felt like celebrating. Not sharing his girlfriend with his roommate.

Huh. Girlfriend. When did he start calling Megan his girlfriend, even in his head? He'd always said they were dating or something, or called her the girl he was seeing if he referred to her to anyone who didn't know her. Otherwise he just called her Megan. Sometimes, when he was feeling playful, he called her his little roomie.

Pushing his thoughts away, he stepped over to Megan, draping his arm around her shoulders. Matt looked up and gently disentangled himself from Megan, his other hand coming up to rub over his mouth. The bastard was trying not to grin outright, like he thought he knew that Chris was jealous.

He squeezed Megan a little closer. She seemed oblivious to their byplay. "Ready?"

She looked up at him and smiled. "Let's go."

"Whoa!" Megan flung out a hand, apparently finding it difficult to make it up their walkway without tripping on the cracks in the cement.

Chris chuckled to himself and caught her by the arm. "I've got you. I won't let you fall."

She beamed up at him, her dark curls falling away from her face, her brown eyes a little glazed and unfocused in the light cast from the streetlamp. They'd had fun at the afterparty. Megan more so than him, but drinking with her was always fun, even if he had to stay sober. He'd made sure that she alternated with water more by the end of the night so she wasn't too drunk to function and wouldn't have a killer hangover in the morning.

They'd danced for a while. It was nice going to a party with her and not having to watch random dudes groping her ass while she danced. He was the only one who had that pleasure tonight. And for a while to come if he had anything to say about it. They'd spent the last hour or so hanging out with friends on the couch, Megan snuggled in his lap. He could get used to that. A little more easily than he'd ever expected. Lance had been there with Abby, who'd looked like she was falling asleep on his shoulder. Every so often Lance glanced at Chris and Megan appraisingly and would look like he was fighting back a smile. It made Chris want to wipe the look off his face, but he'd decided to be the better man and just ignore him when he did it. For now. He might have to punch him once, just on principle.

Once they were inside the house, Megan turned on him, pushing him back against the door, clutching handfuls of his sweatshirt in her little fists. He was surprised enough that he didn't resist. When she slammed herself against him and yanked his head down to hers with a hand on the back of his neck, he was totally on board.

He ran his hands down her back, gripped her ass, and pulled her tightly against him. She squirmed like she couldn't get close enough. He agreed. They were both wearing way too many clothes—pants, sweatshirt, t-shirt, underwear—and that was just him. Megan had on a sexy little red sweater and a pair of jeans. The sweater was soft, and he enjoyed running his hands over it, but not as much as her bare skin.

He pulled back just a little to catch his breath. She didn't want to let him have any room, though, pulling him down and going up on tiptoes at the same time to try not to let him get away. He chuckled against her mouth. "Bed. Now."

She pulled him down hard once more, fusing their lips together, sweeping her tongue into his mouth. He could taste the sweetness of soda laced with a hint of liquor, remnants of Jack and Coke, Megan's drink of choice. He couldn't hold back the smile that was fighting to take over anymore, ruining their kiss. Megan pulled back with a slight sound of annoyance, turned, and started for her bedroom. He could just see her pulling her sweater over her head in the dim living room as she went.

She cast a look back over her shoulder at him, now in just a cami and jeans. "Coming?"

His smile grew wider, and he adjusted himself in his jeans. He'd never had sex with Megan when she'd been drinking. She didn't drink much around the house, apparently saving that for parties. This looked like it was going to be fun. She wasn't passive normally, but she'd never been this aggressive before. And that come-hither look before walking away with extra sway to her hips had him feeling like he might come in his pants.

Chris stripped his sweatshirt and t-shirt off together and tossed them to the side when he got in the room. Megan was lighting a couple of candles. Nice. She wasn't so drunk that she was going to just pass out on the bed, then. He congratulated himself for making her drink water too. He didn't know what he'd do if she got him all ready to go like this and passed out.

Well, yeah he did. He'd go jerk off in the shower and cuddle in next to her after he undressed her. Then they'd finish in the morning. After she finished puking, anyway. This way, they could have fun now *and* in the morning. So much better. And hopefully she wouldn't need to puke either.

He was naked by the time she finished lighting the candles on her dresser and nightstands and put the lighter back in the drawer where she kept it. She still had her clothes on. She walked slowly around the bed to him. Her heavy-lidded eyes raked over him, taking him all in.

He palmed his cock with one hand and watched her make her way over to him. "You seem to be overdressed."

She hummed in agreement. "Wanna help me with that?"

He stepped closer to her, his hands going to her hips. Bending his head, he took her mouth, pulling the fabric of her cami up so he could run his hands underneath. He skimmed his palms up her rib cage and enjoyed the softness of her skin and the way she shivered under his touch. His fingers encountered an elastic band and slid underneath. Megan wasn't wearing a bra. She broke the kiss and raised her arms, letting him pull her top off, now bare from the waist up.

Chris's hands immediately went to her breasts. Cupping them, holding them up so his mouth could devour them. Megan arched her back, giving him full access to her. When he broke away she had her head thrown back and her eyes closed, her face flushed with arousal. He straightened and let his hands fall to her waist where he undid her jeans and pushed them down.

Megan was always responsive, but with just enough alcohol in her to be a little drunk, she was completely uninhibited. He was loving this and couldn't wait to see what other reactions he could get. She helped get her jeans and underwear all the way off and kicked them to the side, her eyes never leaving his. With one hand she reached out and stroked over his chest, down his abs. The other hand joined it, stroking up and behind his neck. With one hand stroking his cock, she pulled his head down for another searing kiss, their tongues dueling, both of them fighting for control.

With her this aggressive and responsive, Chris was so turned on he was afraid he wouldn't last long if she kept stroking him. He ran his hands down her arms, gripped her wrists, and gently pried her hands away from him, taking control of the kiss and the pace. He pinned her hands behind her back again, like he had that first night they got together to stop her from hitting him. This time she didn't struggle against him, and her breasts rubbed against his chest in a move that was deliberate and provocative. He pushed her back toward the bed, making her stumble, and letting her go so she would fall to the bed. She sat down heavily but stopped herself from laying all the way back, her lips curved in a sexy smirk, her eyes dancing with mischief.

She reached forward to grab his cock again, but he caught her hand, not sure what she was trying to do, but sure he wanted to be in charge now. He'd let her have her turn later. Her other hand came up and reached for him, and he caught that one as well. Using his body and his hold on her, he pushed her back all the way. He held her hands pinned down while he took her mouth. She struggled against his hold, but he didn't let up until she relaxed and just kissed him back.

He pulled back and grinned down at her, then transferred one of her hands so he held them both in one hand pinned above her head. "I got you."

"What are you going to do with me?" Her voice was a little breathless with anticipation.

His grin grew wider. "Whatever I want." Without waiting to see what her response might be, he dipped his head again, kissing her neck, working his way down over her collarbone to her breast. He stayed there for a while, enjoying the little gasps and breathless moans he elicited from her with his teasing.

"Chris."

The sound of his name on her lips brought his eyes to her face, his mouth still on her nipple. He sucked it, flicking the tip with his tongue. "Hmm?"

She gasped again. "Chris, please."

He released her nipple from his mouth and brought his head up to look in her face. "Please what?"

She squirmed. "Please fuck me. Now."

"Soon." He turned his attention back to her breasts and she groaned. Smiling against her skin, he finally released her hands, unable to continue holding them while he kissed his way down her body. He settled himself between her thighs and ran his hands down her legs to grip her ankles, moving her feet so they were flat on the bed, forcing her knees to bend and spread wider for him. He ran his hands down her thighs to her waiting sex, her pussy spread and wet with arousal. Just for him.

He started slow, licking with the flat of his tongue, never spending too much time focused on any one area, teasing her. He held her down with his hands on her hips. She was getting impatient, though, and soon her hands were in his hair, grinding his face into her. Knowing what she wanted, he pulled back enough that he could slide two fingers inside her—eliciting another groan followed by a whimper—then sucked her clit into his mouth. Seconds later she exploded around him, her muscles clenching on his fingers, her hands clutching his hair so tightly that it stung his scalp while he helped her ride out her orgasm.

Sitting up on his heels, he reached for a condom on the nightstand. Megan watched him roll it on, her arms and legs splayed, still limp from her orgasm. He watched her watching him, enjoying the undiminished lust still on her face. Once the condom was on, Chris didn't waste any time. He nudged her thighs a little with his knees to make room for himself and surged inside her. Megan's legs immediately went around his waist, her ankles hooking behind his back. He loved when she did that, loved how it made him feel wanted, welcomed, home.

He'd never much cared for missionary position or its variations before. But with Megan it was different. Everything was different. So different it almost started to scare him.

Pushing those thoughts aside, he bent his head to kiss her, thrusting his tongue into her mouth while he thrust his cock into her pussy again and again. She met him thrust for thrust, her gasps and sighs letting him know she was getting close again. He broke their kiss, wetting his thumb with his mouth. A slight shift allowed him to reach between them, his thumb finding her clitoris. She arched against him and the combined friction inside and outside pushed her over the edge again. He pulled her legs up and plunged in as deep as he could once and again, prolonging her orgasm which set off his own release.

He collapsed on the bed next to her, pulling her tight against him and dropping a kiss on her shoulder.

"Wow." Megan still sounded out of breath. He couldn't help his self-satisfied smile. "That was …"

She trailed off and he lifted his head to look down at her, an eyebrow lifted in question. "That was …?"

"Yeah, that was … amazing. I love … the way you make me feel."

Something had flickered across Megan's face, but it was gone before he could decipher it. He looked down in her eyes, still heavy lidded, but no longer glassy with alcohol or lust. "I love the way you make me feel, too."

When she relaxed against him, he realized she'd tensed up. What was that all about? He kissed her briefly on the mouth and got up to take care of the condom. When he came back out of the bathroom, Megan had gotten under the covers and rolled over.

He smiled to himself again. As much as she'd had to drink followed by enthusiastic sex, no wonder she was tired. He climbed into bed behind her, pulled her against him, and fell asleep as well.

Chapter Twelve

Megan woke up the next morning with Chris's arm wrapped around her and his chest pressed against her back. His morning erection poked into the small of her back. Her mouth felt dry, but her stomach and head were okay, which was a rare experience after a party. Chris had made sure she drank lots of water, which meant she hadn't drunk as much alcohol, and the water counteracted what she'd had enough to stave off a hangover. What it also did was make her need to pee like a racehorse.

She slid out from under Chris's arm and made her way to the bathroom. She decided to brush her teeth to get rid of the sticky, post-drinking aftertaste. The other thing about not having a hangover meant that the entire night before was crystal clear in her mind.

Including the fact that she'd almost told Chris that she loved him.

Spitting in the sink and rinsing her mouth again, Megan chastised herself for her stupidity. Some mind-blowing sex and she was about to declare love to the guy. Okay, it wasn't just about the sex, though that was pretty great. It was the way he would sit and study with her, even though she knew he hated it. The way he'd pull her in for a kiss when he saw her no matter where they were or who was around. Once she'd even bumped into him with a bunch of his teammates after her PE class, and he'd stopped mid-conversation to come over just to say hi and kiss her before she went to her next class. He was more considerate than she'd ever expected, both in and out of the bedroom. How was it that this sweet guy was the same one that just had random hook-ups at parties before now?

The combination of alcohol and back to back orgasms had loosened her tongue, and she'd almost spilled her feelings. She'd managed to cover it quickly enough that he hadn't seemed to notice, thank God. She didn't want to scare him off already. But if she wanted to survive this relationship without being destroyed, she needed to rein in her feelings. Though she suspected it might be way too late for that already.

She looked at herself in the mirror. "Fuck."

"Everything alright?" Chris pushed the door open and popped his head in.

She forced a smile on her lips. "Yeah, fine. Why?"

"You don't usually say fuck for no reason." He'd opened the door all the way and propped himself against the frame with his arms crossed over his chest.

Megan shrugged. "I just remembered that I have a big assignment due tomorrow that I've barely started." That wasn't entirely true. She'd been working on her project for her art class for a while, but that was a believable reason to be cursing at herself in the mirror first thing on a Sunday morning.

Chris's eyebrows went up. "You? Forgot an assignment? I better write this down. I don't think that's ever happened before."

"Haha." She smacked him on the arm and pushed him out of the doorway so she could get through. "It's not that I forgot, I just lost track of the date. I was going through my weekly schedule in my head and realized that my figure studies are due tomorrow. I've got some of it done, but I need to finish it today."

Chris pulled her into his arms, and she couldn't help relaxing against him. The skin of his chest was warm against her cheek, and he dropped his head to nuzzle her hair. "Since you're behind on an assignment, which seems crazy to me, do you need to get working on it right away, or can you spend a little time with me first?"

She lifted her face, accepting the kiss he pressed to her lips. "I think I have some time. I'm not that behind. It was just something that I'd forgotten I need to do today."

"Good." He touched his lips to hers again and again, sprinkling light, teasing kisses on her mouth, then down her jaw to her ear, where he nipped at the lobe before he sucked it into his mouth. She gasped and her core clenched from the attention. Who would've thought earlobes were an erogenous zone? No one had ever done that to her before him, and damn, it was hot.

Chris lifted his head and stepped back, leading her back to the bed where he sat down, his cock hardening again after having come down from its typical morning wood. He grabbed a condom and rolled it on before he pulled her against him so that she straddled his lap. He continued pressing light kisses over her collarbones and down the valley between her breasts. He cupped her breasts with both hands and held them so he could lavish them with attention from his mouth, alternately sucking, flicking, and biting the sensitive tips until she felt like she couldn't take anymore.

Megan clutched his head to her chest, grinding against his cock and letting the tip bump against her clit. She felt like she could come just from that and him teasing her breasts. He slipped one hand between them, angled himself at her entrance, and she slid down, her breath catching in her throat as he filled her. He wrapped his arms around her, holding her close, his head resting just above her breasts.

They stayed like that, joined together but still for a moment and relished the connection between them. Then Megan began to move, slowly at first, but picking up speed. She held on to Chris's shoulders and used him for leverage, lifting, dropping, grinding against him, his hands on her hips to guide her. Soon he was pushing against her as well, his hands on her hips pulling her down with more force so that he hit her just right both inside and out. Once again, when she was getting close he slipped his hand between them, his thumb circling her clit, providing the right amount of friction to send her over the edge, with him following close behind.

"Why are you drawing Matt?" Chris had come into the living room after taking a quick shower to find Matt on the couch playing video games and Megan sitting cross-legged on the floor with a sketch pad.

She glanced up at him. "I'm finishing my project that's due tomorrow. I told you about it already, remember?"

"Your homework is drawing pictures of Matt?"

"Yup." She popped the p, then stopped and looked up at him, mischief dancing in her eyes. "It's for my figure drawing class. We're supposed to draw someone in their natural habitat, so to speak." She waved a hand at Matt. "I'm drawing Matt. I have to do a series of sketches. This is my last one."

Chris digested this for a moment and tried not to feel jealous that she hadn't chosen him. "Why him, though?"

She gave him a knowing smile. Damn. He was being really transparent. Even Matt snickered on the couch. "Shut up, Matt. I can't draw you very well when you're jiggling like that."

Matt paused the game and looked affronted. "I don't jiggle!" Chris laughed out loud, not even trying to hold it back.

"Call it whatever you want. Moving some to play your game is fine, but when you're laughing or suppressing laughter it changes the tension and lines in your body. Stop it." She turned to Chris. "And you. Stop being ridiculous. Matt was a logical choice. I see him for tutoring and at home, so I have access to him in a variety of spaces, and he doesn't try to jump my bones every time I see him. You would've spent every session trying to see my sketch pad, like you're doing right now, or trying to get in my pants. Neither of which is helpful."

Chris grunted. He didn't want to admit she was right but knew that she was. She narrowed her eyes at him in one final quelling glare and turned back to her sketch pad. He stood off to one side, careful not to block her light, but with a good enough vantage to watch her work. He knew she was an art major, but he'd never watched her work before. It was fascinating to see her bring the image of Matt to life with what looked to him like a few sweeps of her charcoal pencil and some shading here and there. She made it look effortless, though he could see that she was completely absorbed in her work. She'd even managed to capture

Matt's look of triumph when he blew up an enemy outpost on the game he was playing. It was amazing.

He waited until she'd finished to sit down on the couch. She closed her sketch pad and put it away before moving to settle in next to him. Instead he grabbed her hips and sat her down on his lap. She looked at him in surprise, but he just wrapped his arms around her and pulled her against his chest, where he kissed her thoroughly. He only stopped when Matt made a sound of disgust next to them.

"Didn't you guys get enough of each other this morning?"

Chris smirked. "Nope." He kissed Megan once more before he pulled back. "I had no idea how good of an artist you are."

"Really? You've been looking at my stuff for weeks." She gave him a quizzical look.

"What are you talking about?"

She rolled her eyes. "The paintings in my room?"

It rankled a little that she called it her room and not their room, but Chris decided not to dwell on that and focus on the important part of what she'd said. "You painted those?"

"Yes." She was laughing at him now.

He stood up, dumping her back on the couch. He went into their room—her room—and actually looked at the artwork hanging on the walls. Some of them were famous prints, but the rest were originals. He'd noticed that, he just hadn't realized they were *her* originals.

"Holy shit, Megan. Those are awesome." He settled himself against the doorway with his arms crossed.

Megan met his gaze, but her face was sad. "Thanks. It's nice that someone thinks so."

"What does that mean?" Matt had paused his game and looked at her now, joining in the conversation.

She shrugged and drew her knees into her chest. "My parents don't approve of my pursuing art as a degree. To be honest, they don't approve of me in general."

Chris frowned. Her family didn't approve of her? "Why not?"

She hugged her knees tighter, not looking at either him or Matt. "They're conservative and religious. They don't like that I'm going to a secular school, pursuing what they consider a frivolous and worldly major, and not living with them." She did raise her eyes then. "They don't approve of parties or drinking, and they're not aware of the extent of my involvement with either of those things. And they definitely wouldn't approve if they knew I lived here."

"You didn't tell them you moved?" That was Matt again.

"Well, I told them I moved and gave them the address, but I didn't tell them that I'm not living with Abby anymore, or that I'm living with two guys, and I definitely haven't told them that I'm now sleeping with one of my roommates." She gave Chris a wan smile before she dropped her eyes again and started picking at the fabric of the couch.

Chris let his head drop for a moment and suppressed the clenching in his gut. She didn't want to tell her parents about them? Was she embarrassed that she was with him? "You haven't told them you're seeing someone?" He tried to keep his voice unconcerned, but it came out a little strangled, especially on the last word.

Megan raised her eyes again. "It's not like that, Chris." She pressed her lips together, her nostrils flaring, and gave her head a little shake. "I haven't talked to them much in general. I don't tell them about my life. It's exhausting constantly trying to fend off their disapproval. The only reason they know my major is because I registered for my first semester before I moved out and they saw the forms declaring my major. They don't know that I have a marketing minor, even, so that I can learn how to make it as a solo artist. They don't teach that stuff in the art department, you know." She gave him another little smile, but it still looked forced.

Chris nodded, letting his head drop again. He felt stupid for being so upset about her not telling her parents about them. Her reasons made sense, but the disappointment churning in his gut wouldn't go away. Megan's hands on his chest had him lifting his head, looking down into her brown eyes.

"Hey. Do you tell your parents everything? Have you told them about us?"

"Yes." His voice croaked, dammit. He cleared his throat and tried again. "Yeah, I told them a while ago."

The sincerity in her eyes turned to surprise for just a moment. "Oh." She apparently hadn't expected him to say that. Why wouldn't he tell his parents about her? They were together pretty much anytime they were both free. It would be hard to tell his parents anything without her coming up at some point. His eyes widened as he realized what she was getting at. She didn't tell her parents anything. At all.

"So what do you talk about with your parents?"

She shrugged. "Not much. They try to guilt me into moving back home or changing my major to something they think is more suitable like nursing or elementary ed, and I make appropriate noncommittal noises for a few minutes, and then we hang up. I try to keep conversations as short as possible so they know

I'm alive and well, but I don't tell them much of anything about my life. It's not worth the hassle." He nodded. Her eyes searched his face with something like wonder. "Do you really tell your parents everything?"

"Pretty much."

"Even that you're not planning on graduating?"

He sucked in a breath at that. No, he hadn't told them that yet. He knew they'd be disappointed and he couldn't figure out how to tell them. It didn't seem like a good phone conversation topic.

"What? Is she serious? You're really not graduating? I know you said something about that a few weeks ago, but you've been studying so I thought you'd changed your mind. Why the fuck aren't you graduating?" Matt's words pierced their little bubble and reminded Chris they weren't alone.

He ran a hand over his face. He'd been avoiding this conversation with Matt on purpose. There were enough people nagging him about this shit. He didn't need one more. "Thanks, Megan. Way to throw me under the bus."

She just grinned at him and moved back to the couch. He snorted before turning to Matt. "Yeah, she's serious. At this point I'm not going to graduate."

Matt stared at him, stone-faced. "Okay. And your answer to the last question? Why the fuck not?"

"Why bother?" Chris tried to act nonchalant, like it didn't matter, but his gut was churning and he felt sick thinking about it. Since he'd started studying with Megan he'd begun to wonder what it might take to graduate in the spring. But he'd need to pass this semester, and even with the studying he'd been doing he still wasn't sure he could pull it off.

"Why bother?" Matt scrubbed his hands over his face and muttered to himself. Chris couldn't make out what he was saying, but Megan seemed to find it funny judging by the look on her face. Finally, Matt calmed down enough to talk intelligibly. "Dude. You've been here for almost four and a half years. You're just going to throw it away? Seriously?"

Chris looked away. "I'm not sure I can make it happen. I think my grades have slipped too far this semester."

"I could help you if you want." Chris and Matt both swiveled to look at Megan, where she sat perched on the arm of the couch. She was looking at Chris. "Find out from your professors this week what you'd need to do to pass. We can make it happen if you're serious. We can plan out what you need to do to graduate in May."

Chris sucked in a breath and thought about it. "Really? You think I can do it?"

Megan nodded. "Yeah. We're not quite halfway through. Unless you've failed every single thing you should be able to pull a passing grade. Maybe some of your professors will let you redo stuff that you've failed since you miss so many classes for football. That might work in your favor. Your coaches care about your grades, so if it looks like you're failing anything, see if they can help you work something out. If you're serious, I think we could make it happen."

Hope blossomed in Chris's chest at the determination in Megan's eyes. She really believed he could do it. Most people just assumed he was a dumb jock. Academics had never been his thing. The only reason he'd gone to college was so he could play football. But if she thought he could do it, maybe he could.

"Okay." He nodded once. "Okay, I'll see what needs to be done."

Chapter Thirteen

"Thanks for letting me come hang out tonight. I needed to escape." Megan plopped down on their old couch next to Abby. She'd come over after classes on Thursday evening. "What did you tell Lance?"

Abby shrugged, picking up the remote for the DVD player. "Just that we needed a girls' night. He said he'd go hang with the guys. They'll probably fart and drink beer and play video games. I'm sure they'll all have a blast."

"If I'd known it was that easy, I'd have insisted on this sooner." Megan grabbed a handful of popcorn, munching on it while Abby started the movie.

"So, what are you escaping from? Is everything okay?" Worry seeped into Abby's question despite her attempt at nonchalance.

"Yeah, everything's fine. It's just been a busy week." Abby looked at her expectantly, waiting for more. Megan let out a sigh. "Chris said that I could help him come up with a plan to graduate, and, y'know, help him actually pass his classes. All that on top of my regular work load and tutoring schedule. He's more behind than I expected."

Abby blinked a couple times. "I didn't realize Chris was in danger of not graduating."

"Yeah, I guess he'd decided not to even try anymore, so he barely went to his classes the first few weeks. Just enough to not get dropped for too many absences."

"Wow. Is he going to be able to turn things around?"

Megan rubbed her eyes. "Yeah, I think so. He's been going more lately since I make him study with me, so he's not as behind as he would've been."

Abby threw her arm around Megan's shoulders and gave her a squeeze. "Aw, you're a good influence on him. That's so sweet."

Megan threw popcorn at her. "Shut up."

"Hey! Don't make a mess on my couch!"

"You deserved it. And anyway, it was our couch first."

"Like that matters. Just because you used to be part-owner of the couch doesn't mean you can make it messy now." Abby paused, her attention pulled back to *Mean Girls* playing on the TV. They'd both seen it a million times, so they didn't need to pay attention. After a minute she refocused on Megan. "Seriously, though. I'm glad. He really is a good guy. I'd hate to see him give up on himself. I'm glad you're a good influence on him. How did you get him to agree to try anyway?"

Megan snorted. "Chris got jealous that I was sketching Matt for my figure drawing class."

"Who knew Chris could be so possessive?"

"I know, right? Anyway, it came up that my parents generally disapprove of me. I mentioned that we barely talk and that I hadn't told them that I was living with the two of them, much less that Chris and I are … well, whatever it is that we are."

Abby's eyes narrowed and her gaze sharpened on Megan. "Whatever you are? I thought it was pretty clear by now."

Megan shrugged, trying for indifference, but refusing to meet Abby's eyes and ignoring the statement. "He was upset that I hadn't told my parents about him and said he'd told his parents about me, which surprised me, but when I asked if he'd told his parents he wasn't graduating, he got all quiet." She looked up at Abby, suppressed laughter in her voice. "Man, Matt was pissed when he found out Chris was just going to drop out after this semester." Abby's lips were compressed, and Megan could tell she wanted to say something, but she kept going before Abby could jump in. "So, I told him I'd help him and he agreed." She reached for a handful of popcorn and returned her attention to the movie.

"He told his parents about you?"

Megan lifted one shoulder, still eating popcorn. "That's what he said. Weird, huh?"

Abby's hand reached into the bowl between them. "It's something alright." Megan held her breath while she waited for Abby to say something else about it, and let out a relieved sigh when she didn't.

"Is this the first time you'd told him about your parents?"

Megan shrugged. "Yeah." She gave Abby a pointed look. "You know I don't like talking about them, and," a smirk split Megan's face, "we don't exactly do a lot of talking, if you know what I mean." Megan snickered at the look of disgust on Abby's face.

"TMI, friend. TMI." Abby gave her an acerbic look. "Maybe you guys should try talking a little more. Shouldn't your boyfriend know the details about your family issues?"

"Ah, yes. Well, that was kind of my point earlier. I'm not sure if Chris even considers himself my boyfriend, so ... yeah."

Abby stopped the movie that they were mostly ignoring anyway. "Wait, what? You guys have been together for like a month. Why wouldn't he consider himself your boyfriend? Did you break up? Is that why you're really here?"

"No, nothing like that." Megan started picking at the arm of the couch, pulling off little bits of fuzz where it had pilled. "We just have kind of a casual arrangement. We're exclusive with each other, but neither of us have used those words. Like I said, we don't talk a whole lot, and when we do, I'm not going to bring up something that's more than likely going to have him running for the hills." When Abby didn't answer, Megan stopped picking at the couch and looked at her.

Abby tugged at her lower lip, her eyes on the TV, but unfocused. Finally she pulled herself out of her thoughts and faced Megan. "Let's walk through this. You and Chris are sleeping together, right?"

"Right."

"I don't just mean having sex. I mean actually sleeping in the same bed every night."

"When he's not out of town, yeah."

"Okay. And you're exclusive, meaning neither of you is dating or having sex with anyone else, right?"

"Yeah. I insisted on that from the beginning."

Abby arched an eyebrow. "Oh, so you can talk about your relationship with him that much, but you can't figure out if he's your boyfriend or not?" Megan glared at her, but Abby ignored it. "Do you do things besides just have sex? I mean, I know you said you don't talk much, but surely you don't just have sex. Right?"

Megan laughed. "No, we do other things. He hangs out with me while I do homework, and at least pretends to do homework as well. If he's going to graduate he'll have to do more than just pretend, though." She waved a hand. "Anyway. We have dinner together sometimes, and the three of us hang out and watch movies or play video games every once in a while. Between practices and away games, they're gone a lot, though."

"I hate to break it to you, but I think most people would say he's your boyfriend."

Megan grabbed another handful of popcorn, spilling some with the force of her hand diving into the bowl. "What's the big deal? Why does everything need a label? You refused to call Lance your boyfriend for like two months."

Abby shrugged. "That was different. He was leaving, and I had no expectation of him coming back. I was trying to protect myself."

"That worked out really well, didn't it?" Abby threw a handful of popcorn at Megan. Megan picked a kernel off her shirt and popped it into her mouth. "What happened to not making a mess of your couch?"

"I said *you* couldn't make a mess of it. It's my couch. I can cover it in popcorn if I want. You can't compare your relationship with Chris to mine with Lance, though. The fundamental basis for the relationship is different."

Megan sighed and glared at Abby again. "I came here to get away from the headaches of my life, not have you add to them."

"Well, one thing's the same at least."

"What's that?"

"You're in denial as much as I was."

Megan threw popcorn back at Abby, who just laughed and turned the movie back on. Abby was right, though. She was denying the depth of her feelings about Chris. She was just starting to acknowledge them herself. There was no way she'd tell Chris how she felt, so why bother telling Abby? She'd learned over the years that there was no use voicing

your desire for something that couldn't happen. It
wouldn't change anything, and it only made you hurt
more.

A wolf-whistle sounded from the direction of the
kitchen when Megan walked out of her bedroom. Matt
stood there in a snug fitting vest and cargo pants, a toy
bow in one hand, and a quiver of arrows sticking out
over his shoulder. "Looking good."

"Get your own woman!" Chris pushed Matt out
of his way with his Captain America shield to get out
of the kitchen while Matt just laughed. Chris stood in
the doorway, his eyes raking over Megan in her black
skinny jeans, knee high boots, and fitted black leather
jacket. She'd used some washout dye to turn her dark
brown curls auburn to complete her Black Widow
costume. It wasn't quite the right shade, but it was the
closest she could get. She pulled the toy gun out of the
holster on the cargo belt slung around her hips and
blew across the tip.

His eyes darkened and he stalked across the room,
pulling her tight against him. Megan chuckled when
her hands encountered the fake foam muscles under

the fabric of his costume. "I don't think you need the extra help with the physique."

He grinned down at her. "Thanks for the compliment, but I couldn't find one without the muscles. You ready to go?"

She nodded and he pulled her in for a kiss before they all piled into Matt's car. They'd played rock, paper, scissor earlier to decide who would be the DD and Matt had lost. They were on their way to the team's annual costume party that they held every October. This year they got to have it on Halloween, since it fell on the Saturday of the only weekend before Thanksgiving that they didn't have a game.

Megan had been looking forward to it since they'd all decided to go as characters from *The Avengers*. She'd never been part of a group costume. When the guys had suggested it, she'd been doubtful. She hadn't seen the movie before, which had made them groan in disbelief and determine to remedy the situation at the first opportunity. She'd enjoyed the movie more than she'd expected to, and started trying to figure out how to put together a costume for Black Widow almost as soon as the movie had ended.

Chris had sprung for a store-bought costume, saying that it would take too much time and too much work to put one together himself. She and Matt had managed to find most of the stuff they needed at thrift

stores. She'd scored with the jacket. It was perfect—
black leather that zipped up the front with an almost
non-existent stand up collar. It had only cost twenty
dollars, and she could wear it for more than just
Halloween. The other bonus was that she wouldn't
freeze in this costume on the cold, rainy night.

They went to the same house where the pool
party had been at the beginning of the semester, the
party already well underway. So much had changed
since she'd been here last. The weather meant there
wouldn't be any swimming going on tonight and more
of the house was opened for the partiers. Like last time,
there was a variety of drinks available, plus bowls of
Halloween candy placed all around.

Megan took it all in, not recognizing as many
people as she expected due to their costumes. She was
less recognizable than normal as well, with her hair the
wrong color. A young woman in a skirt suit turned,
and Megan almost did a double take. "Abby?"

Abby grinned and rushed over, giving her a hug,
lightly touching Megan's curls. "Hey! I almost didn't
recognize you with your hair like this. I like it!"

Megan laughed. "I know what you mean. I've
never seen you dressed like this before."

"Well, I'm Pepper Potts, so I have to look the
part." She pulled out her phone, put on a serious face,
and pretended to check it. "Mr. Stark will be with you

in a moment." Her serious face broke into a grin, and she turned to grab the tall guy in a leather jacket behind her. When he turned, Megan saw Lance sporting a goatee, a t-shirt under his jacket with a glowing ring in the center of his chest.

He pulled sunglasses down his nose and looked her up and down over the top of them. "Nice to see you, Black Widow."

"Nice to see you too, Mr. Stark." Megan couldn't help but laugh at him. He chuckled as well before he pulled Abby to his side and bent down to kiss her.

Chris appeared at her elbow, drinks in hand. He handed one to her before taking in Lance and Abby's costumes. "Nice. You guys look perfect."

They talked and laughed together as a group for a while before Matt drifted off on his own. The two couples took to the dance floor, the alcohol loosening up Abby enough that she danced for more than one song, though she and Lance wandered off long before Megan and Chris were done.

The team took their costume party seriously, which explained why the guys had been so insistent that she dye her hair, and Chris wasn't willing to go for a cheap DIY version of Captain America. They hosted it every year on their free weekend, regardless of how close it was to Halloween. The team managers acted as judges for the costume contest. They were entered into the group costume category.

Eventually it was time for the costumes to be judged. She and Chris split up to find the other three members of their group so they could meet in the entryway before going in. Megan made a pass through the kitchen, then down the back hallway, checking out the bathroom line and listening for recognizable voices next to the bedrooms. She felt like a creeper, but didn't want to walk in on random people hooking up, so she just tried to determine if the voices in the occupied rooms belonged to any of her people as quickly as possible before she moved on.

With no sign of Lance and Abby or Matt, she wandered back toward the living room. She spotted a Captain America across the room near the entryway, a blonde chick dressed as a slutty devil wrapping her arms around his waist from behind. His back was to her. Huh. She hadn't noticed more than one Captain America here earlier. But Chris wouldn't let some random chick wrap herself around him like that. Would he?

Captain America turned, his hands on the slutty devil's arms. Megan sucked in a breath, her gut clenching. Chris laughed and looked down at the girl, his hands still on her arms. The girl went up on tiptoe, obviously trying to kiss him, but he turned his head and she got his cheek.

"You know it's just a matter of time, right?"

Megan ripped her eyes away from the scene unfolding in front of her, Chris with his hands on someone else and not flinging her away in disgust. Turning to the owner of the voice, she saw a redhead dressed as a Playboy bunny, with a black corset and white bunny ears on her head. Normally Megan would've laughed at the cliché, but she was too shocked and confused to say anything but, "What?"

The bunny nodded toward Chris and the blonde she-devil. His hands were still on her shoulders, but he'd set her away from him. His expression was hard to read with half his face covered.

"Until he dumps you and moves on. I'm shocked you've lasted as long as you have."

Megan looked at the bunny again, who ran her eyes up and down Megan's body, the look on her face one of condescending judgment. The talking cliché continued before Megan could respond, her neurons still firing on a time delay. "I can only imagine he started fucking you because you live in their house. I can't blame him. With the football season being what it is, these guys don't have time for chasing skirts as much as during the rest of the year. But he doesn't do relationships." She smirked. "You're sweet, but don't get too attached."

With that, she flounced off, her fluffy tail bobbing behind her with the sway of her hips, leaving Megan and her brain to catch up with what had just happened. But she couldn't. Couldn't process this. When she looked back into the living room, Chris and the she-devil were nowhere to be seen. She didn't know what that meant. He hadn't kissed her, so she didn't think he was in a back room fucking her.

God, that would be humiliating. Chris wouldn't do that to her, right? They'd agreed that they'd break up when one of them wanted to move on. He hadn't done anything to make her doubt him before now. Sure, girls were always swarming him at parties, but he'd always given them his charming smile and then found Megan. He hadn't found her yet. Bile rose in Megan's throat. They were supposed to be looking for the other three. Maybe that's what Chris was doing. She didn't want to think about this anymore.

Liquor. She needed liquor. Now.

She turned and pushed her way through the crowd to the kitchen. Once there she pulled one of the tiny Solo cups off a stack and set it down. The guy manning the liquor waited for her to pick from the available options.

"Tequila."

He nodded and filled the little cup. She knocked it back, closing her eyes against the burn of the liquor going down her throat.

She set the cup down. "Again."

After two more shots, she felt a touch on her arm and turned to see Chris looking down at her. "There you are."

She blinked at him, not sure what he meant. The echo of the bunny's words blocked out thought and understanding. What if that redheaded bunny was right? What if he were only with her out of convenience? For all she knew, he made every girl he was with feel like the most important one in the world while he was with her. It was after he was done that reality came crashing in.

"Megan? Are you okay?" There was concern on his face.

She didn't know what to think or how to act, so she forced a smile. "Yeah, fine. Why?"

His eyes stood out behind his blue mask, examining her face. "Everyone else is at the front. It's time for the costume contest. You're the only one missing." He cast a glance around the kitchen. "Did you get thirsty?"

"Something like that." She forced a short laugh. It was all she could manage. "When I didn't find anyone,

I thought I'd camp out here and see if they happened by."

"Oh. Okay." She felt like he was trying to look inside her, and she looked away. "Well, like I said, they're all by the front door waiting for us. It's almost time for the judging to start."

Megan nodded, swaying a little when she stood, the three shots of tequila in quick succession on top of the drinks she'd already had making her a little unsteady.

"Whoa, there." Chris caught her arm. "Are you alright?"

She took a breath, steadied herself, and pulled her arm out of his grasp. "Yup. I'm fine. Let's go."

Head high, she strode in front of Chris to meet up with the others. But the excitement she'd felt at the beginning of the night was gone. She didn't care about the stupid costume contest anymore. She just wanted to be alone to sort out her feelings about Chris and how she could be so dumb as to fall in love with him already. He'd never stuck with anyone before. It made sense that he would enjoy having the convenience of someone living with him be his first relationship that lasted longer than a few hours.

But what did they really have in common? Nothing. He was a jock who might not even graduate, and she was an artist. They barely knew anything about each other because they barely talked.

Sure, she was having the best sex of her life, but was that really the basis of a relationship?

How much longer could this go on?

Chapter Fourteen

Chris kept a hand on Megan's back while they walked to meet their friends. Partly because it was normal for him to do that, partly to make sure she didn't fall down. He'd been a little surprised when she stood up and almost lost her balance. Their plan had been to get drunk after the costume contest judging was over. He knew she liked to party and have a good time, but he couldn't figure out why she'd decided to do it on her own. And when she was supposed to be looking for the others.

He froze for a second, remembering the blonde chick who'd accosted him earlier. Had Megan seen that? He hadn't noticed her in the room, but he'd been focused on trying to find the other three. With a mental shrug, he dismissed that as the reason for her change in demeanor. If she'd seen that, then she had to have seen him give the girl the brush off. He tried to let them down easy—he wasn't a complete bastard—but since Megan had entered the picture, he always turned them down.

The only other thing he could think of was that one of the assholes that liked to talk about her had said something to her. Before they reached Lance, Abby, and Matt, he stopped her with a hand on her arm.

"Hey. What's going on? Are you okay?"

Her lips curved up and her teeth became visible in what might have passed for a smile, except it didn't reach her eyes or light up her face like a real smile did. And he was used to seeing her real smiles pretty regularly. "Sure. I'm fine. Why?"

Her brown eyes gazed back at him, guarded. He'd never seen that look on her before. Anger, laughter, desire, yes, but never this wall that kept him from figuring out what was going on in her head. "You started drinking on your own. While you were supposed to be looking for Lance and Abby and Matt. Did someone say something to you or something?"

"Ha ha ha." He thought it was supposed to be a laugh, but it sounded like words. The last time Megan got drunk she'd been extra horny. He guessed that alcohol just amplified whatever feelings she had, which was why she was having such a hard time faking laughter and smiles now. She could block the real feeling, but not be convincing with the cover.

She shook her head at him, that weird fake smile still in place. "No. No one said anything to me. I couldn't find anyone so I thought I'd have a drink or two and see if anyone wandered through the kitchen."

It was such an obvious lie, but he didn't think he'd get the truth out of her in the middle of the party, so he just nodded. "Okay. But you can talk to me if something's bothering you. You know that right?"

She laughed this time. A real laugh, but still without humor. "I'm fine, Chris. No need to worry about little ol' me."

He didn't know how to respond to that, so he just laced his fingers with hers and led her over to where Matt, Lance, and Abby waited for them and watched their conversation. Matt shot him a questioning look, but he just shrugged and smiled, hoping no one would question further. They all seemed to get the message, and they moved as a group into the living room with the other people waiting to be judged.

They ended up getting third place in the group category. First place went to a group of Hogwarts students, and second place was claimed by a trio that came as Han Solo, Luke Skywalker, and Princess Leia.

Despite Matt getting stuck as DD, Chris decided to limit himself. After Megan's weird attitude before the judging, he didn't feel like getting drunk. They'd settled themselves on a couch around a coffee table with a bottle of vodka and the tiny Solo shot cups. Megan seemed to have recovered herself, and she and Lance were playing some kind of drinking game where they took a shot whenever they heard anyone say a particular word. He had no idea what. He wasn't paying that much attention.

Abby sat on the other side of Lance, watching the two drinking and laughing with an amused expression on her face. She got up and moved to sit next to Chris. "Why aren't you joining in? I thought I heard Matt say he was driving."

He shrugged, not sure what to tell her. "Just not in the mood."

She nodded, seeming to accept his non-answer. They chatted for a while, which was nice. He hadn't talked to her much since she and Lance had moved in together. Hell, he'd barely seen her. The only times he had, they'd all gone to parties, and she'd stuck with Lance, while he'd been with Megan. Not a lot of opportunity for conversation.

He threw an arm around Abby's shoulders and pulled her against his side in a hug. "I've missed hanging out with you, Abby. You and Lance should come by sometime."

"Aw, I've missed you, too." She wrapped her arms around his waist and squeezed, smiling up at him. "You guys are so busy this time of year with practices and games and everything. Are you going home for Thanksgiving break? If not, maybe we could do something then. Or one weekend after the season ends at least."

"I'll be heading home, yeah. Maybe I'll come back on Saturday, and we can all hang that night or Sunday."

"That would be great. Lance would like that too. He doesn't say anything, but I think he misses hanging out with you guys."

He smiled back at her, surprised to find himself enjoying a party where he wasn't drinking or scoring with a chick. Megan and Lance were both pretty wasted by this time, giggling and snorting and barely able to stay upright. Chris pulled out his phone and checked the time. Almost midnight. "Whaddaya think,

Abs? Should we drag these two home and put them to bed so they can puke their guts out in the morning?"

Abby surveyed her boyfriend and best friend in all their drunken glory for a moment before she nodded. "Yeah, we should." She cast a look around the room. "Do you want to go find Matt, or should I?"

"I'll stay here with these two if you don't mind. That way if one of them falls over, I can catch them or at least pick them back up."

She laughed and nodded. "Okay. I'll go look for Matt. Wish me luck."

A few minutes later Abby was back with Matt and they headed out to the car. Chris supported Megan, and Matt had one of Lance's arms slung around his shoulders. Lance was singing something off key and seemed to be making up his own lyrics as they went. Matt and Abby both laughed at him, which only made Lance laugh, trip, and sing louder.

They finally made it to Abby's car, where they stuffed Lance in the back seat and both he and Matt gave Abby hugs before she drove off with a promise to call if she needed help getting him into their apartment. She'd assured them that since they lived on the first floor, it wouldn't be too bad. No stairs for him to fall down.

On the way to Matt's car, Matt cast a glance at Chris. "I figured you'd be further gone by now."

Chris shrugged and didn't say anything. Megan was stumbling along beside him, humming to herself, barely keeping up with him. He decided it was more work than it was worth to keep her on her feet and scooped her up in his arms to carry her the rest of the way to the car.

"Hey!" She stiffened at first, but he just squeezed her against his chest. Throwing her arms around his neck, she snuggled in closer to him, humming to herself. A little contented smile played across her lips and she closed her eyes.

Chris couldn't decide what to make of her tonight. And he hoped that she'd remember enough about whatever had upset her to be able to tell him about it tomorrow. With as much as she'd had to drink, he wasn't sure that would be possible.

Cold air on his skin and the sound of retching brought Chris awake. He sat up and ran a hand over his face before he threw back the covers the rest of the way and made his way to the bathroom. Megan must've pulled the covers off his torso in her rush to get to the bathroom. He knelt next to her, holding back her hair with one hand and rubbing her back with the other. She moved her hands away from her face when he gathered her hair in his hand and knelt on the floor clutching the toilet bowl. Her small frame shuddered each time she vomited.

He couldn't help but be grateful that he hadn't gotten drunk last night. The sight and smell of Megan vomiting was almost enough to make him puke as it was, and he didn't have a hangover. If he did, he couldn't imagine how miserable they'd both be.

When she had succeeded in getting everything out, Megan collapsed onto the bathmat on the floor, groaning and clutching her head. He brushed some hair away from her forehead and placed a gentle kiss there. "I'll get you some ibuprofen and a glass of water." He was careful to whisper, and she patted his arm before he got to his feet. He pulled on a pair of shorts before he headed out to the kitchen.

Chris had tried to get her to drink water last night between drinks, but she'd been more belligerent than normal about it and refused, preferring shots more than she usually did. Something was wrong last night, he was sure of it, but he had no idea what. She was fine, and then she wasn't so fast that he felt like he had whiplash. He had no idea how to go about figuring out what happened. She'd refused to tell him anything while they were still at the party, and she'd drunk so much that she'd passed out in the car on the way home. He'd had to strip her out of her clothes, and was a little disappointed that it hadn't gone like he'd hoped when he'd first seen her in her costume. He had planned on peeling everything off of her while she stood panting with arousal, begging him to get inside her. He loved it when she did that, and he liked to tease her until she did as often as possible.

Instead, he peeled the clothes from her while she was mostly unconscious, and the partly conscious part of her smacked at his hands and told him to leave her alone instead of helping. He'd finally gotten her down to her panties (which was a lacy thong, dammit) and tucked her into bed before he'd stripped down and climbed in next to her. He'd lain awake for quite a while, holding her, making sure she didn't vomit in her sleep. He knew she'd had quite a bit to drink, but he wasn't sure exactly how much or how well she could hold her liquor. Apparently pretty well for such a tiny person.

Megan stood at the sink splashing water on her face when Chris came back to their bedroom. He deposited the pills in her outstretched hand and watched her toss them back, drinking just enough water to swallow the pills before setting the cup down on the counter next to the sink. "Thanks for getting that for me."

"No problem." Chris stood in the doorway with his arms crossed and leaned against the doorframe. "Are you done puking for now? You should drink a little more water."

She started to nod, but stopped, holding her head in both hands and letting out a moan of pain. "Nodding is a bad idea."

Chris couldn't help grinning. "I know that feeling. Come here." He reached for her and scooped her into his arms to deposit her back in the bed. He grabbed the glass of water and set it on the nightstand before climbing in with her, pulling her against him so they sat propped up against the headboard, her head resting on his shoulder.

Megan closed her eyes and relaxed against him. She smelled like a distillery, but he didn't mind. He enjoyed the feeling of her body against his, the way she snuggled into him, the simple pleasure of just holding her. More than he had ever expected. They stayed that way for a while. Chris coaxed some more water into her, which she was able to keep down.

After a soft tap on the door, Matt poked his head in. "Hey. I'm going for burritos. You guys want some?"

"Shhh." Megan put one hand over her ear. "Not so loud."

Chris grinned again. "Yeah. Get my usual for both of us." Megan smacked at his chest weakly, shushing him some more. Matt chuckled before he closed the door behind him.

Chris pulled Megan in closer and held her while she dozed off. He'd let her rest and get an egg, bacon, and cheese breakfast burrito in her belly before he tried to figure out what freaked her out the night before. While she seemed totally miserable, he didn't think she'd had enough to drink to make her black out. The real question was, would she talk to him or just pretend like she didn't remember?

Chapter Fifteen

Megan woke up when Chris brushed a kiss across her lips and whispered goodbye. He did it every morning during the week. He had since that first time when he'd woken her up before he left to make sure she had an alarm set. She normally roused a little at his kiss and whispered words, then drifted back to sleep with a smile on her lips.

This time she was awake and couldn't go back to sleep. She still felt groggy and out of sorts from her hangover the day before. Her head didn't hurt and she wasn't nauseated anymore. It was more a lingering feeling of malaise and unhappiness. She didn't party that often during the school year, so she wasn't used to having a hangover linger. Usually it was the headache and faint sense of nausea that stayed into the second day. This felt different, but she couldn't figure out what else it might be.

Chris had been sweet all day yesterday, just hanging out with her, holding her, making sure she drank water. They watched some movies in the evening, and she managed to do a little bit of reading. Not everything, though, which wasn't like her.

She kicked off the covers and decided to get the rest of her homework done since she was awake anyway. Maybe that's what was bothering her. Some sort of guilt for not having finished her homework over the weekend? That seemed unlikely. She was a good student and didn't often blow things off, but she knew how to fake her way through a class when she needed to, especially if all she'd skipped was some reading. If you've read at least the first few paragraphs and skimmed the next several pages you could count on being able to answer one of the first questions a professor asked. If you volunteered a response right away, the professor would be unlikely to just call on you when you weren't prepared. And if all else failed, comment on someone else's comment.

The memory of the party came back to her in the shower. It was always where ideas and stray bits of brain fluff popped up. Showers often jogged memories clouded by alcohol as well. It wasn't uncommon for her to have memory gaps while she was hungover. She'd never had one not get filled in by the end of the next day, though. Today was no different.

She was minding her own business, washing her hair, humming to herself, when wham. That she-devil with her arms around Chris, that bitch of a fake Playboy bunny talking about Chris and his manwhore ways. How he was only with her because she was a convenient hole to stick his dick in. So convenient that they shared a room and a bed.

It hit her like a kick in the gut. The anger. At the she-devil. At the talking bunny cliché. At Chris. At herself. The fear that maybe that jersey chaser was right, that she was nothing more to Chris than a convenient hole. He could be so charming, and he had a reputation for making a girl melt under his undivided attention. He just didn't normally maintain that attention any longer than it took for him to get off and get out. Was that all this was? Sure, it had lasted longer than his normal one hour hookups. But did it amount to little more between them? Were they really just fuck buddies?

And that led her to the final feeling. Disgust. With the whole situation, but mostly with herself. For falling for him when she went into this with no illusion that it would turn into something more, something lasting. How could she have fallen so hard so fast?

Turning, she let the water wash over her, rinsing away the shampoo, then tilted her head back further so the water pounded on her upturned face. "Fuck."

What was she going to do now?

Chris knocked on the open door of the head coach's office and stuck his head in. "Hey, Coach. Coach Riggs said you wanted to talk to me?" The assistant coach had grabbed him at the end of practice, emphasizing that Coach Hanson needed to talk to him before he left.

Coach Hanson looked up from the papers on his desk. "Sure, Watkins. Have a seat." He shuffled the papers around, putting some in a folder and setting it off to the side while Chris dropped his bag on the floor and sat down. Coach Hanson sat back in his chair and watched Chris for a moment before he spoke again. "I wanted to talk to you about graduation eligibility and what you're planning for the future."

Chris shifted a little in his seat. "I'm still passing all my classes."

Coach nodded. "Yeah, for now. Your assigned tutor says you haven't been keeping your appointments with her. You going to be able to maintain your C average?"

"Yeah. My, uh, girlfriend's been helping me with my classes. She's helping me figure out what I need to take next semester so I can graduate."

Coach's blue eyes sharpened at that and he sat forward again, his beefy forearms resting on his desk. "Girlfriend, huh? Is she smart?"

"Yes, sir. She works in the tutoring center. She's the one that you gave special permission for Matt Schwartz to use."

"I thought Schwartz said she was his roommate. Don't you live with him, too?"

"Yes." Chris didn't think it was necessary to elaborate. The man was obviously coming to his own conclusions.

Coach Hanson shook his head a little and let out a low whistle. "She's your girlfriend now, huh? Careful there." He rapped his knuckles on the desk once. "Anyway, glad to hear you've pulled your head out of your ass enough to get serious about school. For a while there I didn't think you were going to finish."

Chris shrugged. "I wasn't planning on it until recently."

"I know you were disappointed that you didn't get an invite to the National Scouting Combine. Have you thought about going to a Regional Combine? You'll be eligible once the season is over at the end of the month."

Chris swallowed, but didn't say anything. Coach Hanson's blue eyes had that look in them like he was trying to read your mind. He always looked like that when you didn't answer fast enough for his liking. He was an intense man. It was part of the reason he made such a good coach.

Finally, Chris shrugged again. "I hadn't really considered it. I figured that if they wanted me they'd send an invite."

Coach Hanson made a dismissive sound. "Watkins, I've never thought you were stupid. I know academics isn't your strongest subject, but that doesn't mean you're an idiot. You go to school in what amounts to the middle of nowhere in a pretty minor division. If you really wanted to be able to get an invite, you should've gone to a school with a bigger program. Or you suck up whatever stupid thing you've got in your head about being too proud to go to a Regional Combine and go after what you want. This is your chance." When Chris didn't immediately respond, Coach kept talking. "There's no shame in going to open tryouts, you know. Plenty of good players started as walk-ons. If you want to go pro, you should do it. You regret the things you don't try more than the things you do."

Coach stared at him and waited for him to respond. Chris wasn't sure what to say, but knew he wouldn't be dismissed until he came up with something. After a long day, he was hungry and tired and just wanted to go home. Thinking about graduation, Regional Combines for the NFL, or what to do beyond cuddling up with Megan and falling asleep wasn't what he wanted right now. He just wanted to leave, but knowing he'd get his ass chewed tomorrow, plus extra speed drills as punishment, kept him in his seat.

He forced his brain to grind out some kind of answer. "I'll think about it."

Coach nodded once. "Good. Do that. Tell me which Combine you plan on registering for by our last game."

Chris's eyes widened, but he didn't say anything in the face of Coach's stare. Instead, he nodded. "Okay."

Coach waved a hand toward the door indicating his dismissal and turned back to the papers he'd stuffed in a folder. Chris collected his bag and headed out, his mind churning with thoughts of the future.

"Charlie? This is unexpected." Megan slid a few more things into her bag, packing up to leave the tutoring center. She'd just finished with her last appointment when her phone rang and flashed her brother's name and the picture she'd taken of him last Christmas when they'd all been home.

"Hey, Megan." His baritone voice carried over her phone, and she could tell he was smiling just from the way he said her name.

She smiled back. "What's up? Did someone die? You never call me." Her tone was half-joking but a niggle of worry squirmed in the back of her mind. They only called each other on their birthdays and major holidays. Since it was November 4, it was neither of those things.

Charlie laughed. "No, everything's fine. A guy can't call his little sister without having a death notification these days?"

"Ha. No. It's just unusual for you to call me out of the blue. How's it going? How's school?" Charlie was at Seattle Pacific University. A year ahead of Megan in school, he would graduate at the end of May.

"Good. Just jumping through all the hoops so I can finish this year. You know how it goes."

Megan pinched her phone between her head and shoulder as she finished gathering her things to head out. "Yeah. I'm not quite there yet. Next year, though."

"Yeah. So've you given any thought to getting your teaching certificate?"

Switching the phone to her left hand, she grabbed her bag and slung it over her right shoulder, heading for the door. "What? No. Why would I do that?"

Silence greeted her question. Finally, with a sigh, "No, I guess not. Why get something you know you could make money with?"

"Seriously, Charlie? You called to lecture me about my life choices? I get enough of that from Mom and Dad." She stopped in the hallway, halfway to the door, frustration tensing her muscles. Her brothers didn't understand her much more than her parents did, though they were usually more tolerant. They were both good little boys that toed the line, Logan, the oldest, had gone to law school and Charlie, fun-loving Charlie, became serious and studious, majoring in theology, with plans of getting his Master of Divinity next. Their parents were so proud of their sons. She was the black sheep, and they constantly tried to bring her back into the fold.

Charlie's sigh carried through the phone. "I just care about you, Megan. I want you to be able to support yourself once you graduate. I just don't think—"

"Yeah, that's the problem." God, she was tired of getting lectured about this. "You don't think. You don't think I can succeed as an artist. You don't think I should blow off Mom and Dad so much. You don't think that I know what I want and have what it takes to get it. You don't think about me." Charlie's disappointment with her was the hardest to take. They'd been so close when they were kids, but had started to grow apart in high school once she began to take her art more seriously. When he'd left to go to college their relationship had fractured further to the strained truce they currently operated under where they saw each other at their parents' house when they both happened to be there and talked on the phone for a few minutes a few times a year.

"Megan, come on."

"No, you come on. Look, I know you don't agree with all of my choices. And that's fine. You don't have to. I don't agree with all of yours, either. But I at least respect your right to make those choices and don't try to pressure you to be different. The least you could do is extend the same courtesy to me."

Charlie blew out another long breath. "You're right. I'm sorry." A few moments passed in silence. Megan wasn't sure what to say, so she didn't say anything. She still didn't know why Charlie had really called. It was a busy week, with two papers due and a major test on Friday, not to mention her ongoing projects for figure drawing and painting. All she wanted was to get off the phone and get home so she could relax for a little while and get started on her homework.

She walked the rest of the way toward the door. The oppressive clouds from earlier in the afternoon had opened up and now it was pouring. Cold and dark and raining like Niagara Falls. "Shit."

"Megan!" Oops, she was still on the phone with her theology-student brother who never cursed.

"Sorry, Charlie. It's pouring out and I have to walk halfway across campus to get to my car to go home."

"At least you have your car today. Don't you usually walk?"

Megan shifted her feet. "Um, didn't Mom and Dad tell you? I moved. I don't live close enough to walk anymore."

"Oh, yeah. Well, do you have an umbrella?"

"No. I didn't bring it today." She let out a long sigh. "Look, I need to go. I don't want to walk through pouring rain on the phone. Did you need to talk to me about something? And if it's an in-depth discussion, can I call you back later?"

Charlie let out a soft chuckle. "Yeah, right. Like you'd actually call me back."

"Charlie, I really don't—"

"No, it's fine. I get it." It was Charlie's turn to interrupt this time. "I was calling to see if you're going to come home for Thanksgiving."

Megan froze, one hand still on the push bar of the door. "Uh, I hadn't really thought about it. I might be going home with a friend."

"With Abby?"

Megan snorted. "No. Come on, Charlie. You know what her mom's like. That Thanksgiving would be worse than one at our house."

"Be nice. Anyway, what friend?"

"Just, y'know. A friend." She was stalling, and doing a terrible job of it. She didn't want to promise to go home, but she hadn't gotten an invite elsewhere yet. It hadn't come up at home, but she was hoping that Chris might invite her to go with him. If he did, that would put some of her doubts to rest. But she didn't want to bring it up. He needed to do it unprompted or it wouldn't mean as much.

"Does this friend happen to be male?" Charlie's voice was overly casual. Megan snorted at his attempt to find out more without trying to be obvious about his insane curiosity.

Megan decided that ignoring the question was the best plan. "I'll think about coming home if I don't get invited elsewhere. I gotta go, Charlie."

"Okay. I know Mom and Dad would really like it if you came."

"I'll think about it. That's the best I can give you right now."

"Fine. I'll talk to you later."

"Okay, sure. Bye." Megan ended the call and stared out the glass doors. The rain hadn't let up at all during the few minutes on the phone with Charlie. She'd hoped it would, but with her luck right now, it wasn't surprising. Busy, crappy week. Unpleasant phone call with her brother that she used to be close to. And a command to come home for Thanksgiving.

It had been issued as an invitation, but she harbored no illusions about the true nature of it. She was sure her parents had put him up to that, hoping that her brother would be able to have more influence over her than they did. He didn't. It was hard to maintain a close relationship with someone who disapproved of your every decision, whether that was her parents or her brothers.

And now Charlie suspected she had a boyfriend. She didn't even know what to do with that, because she wasn't sure where her relationship with Chris stood. That was why it was easier to just dodge Charlie's questions and get off the phone as quickly as possible. More things to think about and figure out. She wouldn't figure it out standing in the entryway of the tutoring center hoping it would stop pouring. Like everything else, she'd just have to suck it up, put her head down, and get through it.

With that thought, she zipped her jacket up as far as it would go, pushed the door open and made her way to her car as fast as she could with her head down and arms crossed, trying to protect herself as much as possible from the rain and the cold raging outside.

Chapter Sixteen

Laughter from the kitchen caused Chris to get off the couch to see what had Matt cracking up.

Matt was almost doubled over, pointing at Megan. "You look like a drowned rat!"

Megan stepped closer to Matt and punched him in the arm before she calmly took off her shoes. Matt was right, though. Her hair was plastered to her face, and he could see where it had dripped all down her neck, making the collar of her t-shirt wet. Her jacket, which was now draped over the back of a kitchen chair to dry, had protected her torso from the worst of the downpour, but couldn't stop the water that drained directly down her neck. Her jeans were soaked through.

Chris crossed his arms and propped his shoulder against the doorway, not saying anything. Matt continued to laugh and Megan glared at him, flipping him off before turning to see Chris blocking her exit.

"Hey." Her voice didn't give anything away. Chris had expected her to sound more pissed off, at least from the way she'd punched Matt and flipped him off. Not that he could blame her. Matt was still chuckling and shaking his head as he went back to making dinner. Instead, she sounded calm, controlled. It was odd. Megan was many things, but controlled was rarely one of them, at least in his experience. She felt things strongly and had no qualms about sharing her opinions and feelings with others, especially with him and Matt.

"Hey." Chris straightened up and held out a hand to her. "Let's get you warm and dry."

She stared at his outstretched hand for a moment, then her eyes flicked to his face, searching. Finally, she cracked a little smile and took his hand. "Sounds good. Thanks."

He led her to their bedroom, leaving her for a moment while he turned on the shower for her. When he went back out to the bedroom, she still stood in the middle of the room where he'd left her. She looked almost lost. Her head was down and the part of her hair not plastered to her face had swung forward, hiding her expression.

He reached out and touched her shoulder. "Hey. I got the shower started for you. Want help undressing?" He gave her a suggestive wink. She laughed, which made him let out his breath in relief. He'd never seen Megan act like this before, and her laughter made him think she was alright after all.

"Help undressing? The shower's too small. You know you can't fit in there with me." Her eyes twinkled back at him, and he gathered her in his arms, uncaring if she got him damp. She rested her head against his chest for a moment before she pulled back, her brows drawn together in consternation. "I left a wet spot."

He shrugged. "It's okay."

She smiled and took a step back, pulling her shirt over her head and tossing it toward the hamper. Her bra followed behind it. She struggled a little more getting her jeans off, the wet denim sticking to her legs. "God, I'm soaked to the skin." She pulled off her panties, tossed them behind her, and headed into the bathroom.

Chris followed her in. She turned just before she stepped into the shower stall and arched an eyebrow at him, a small smile playing over her lips. He grinned back and enjoyed imagining what might be going through her head.

It would be fun to join her in there, but she was right, they wouldn't both fit comfortably. And if he got in, he'd block the water from reaching her, making her cold, and the point of this shower was for her to warm up. Him getting in the way was the last thing she needed. He wouldn't object to helping her finish warming up afterward, though.

The wet spot in the middle of his chest from where she'd rested her wet hair was kind of annoying, so he stripped off the t-shirt. It made it more comfortable to stay in the humid bathroom while the shower filled the tiny room with steam. He sat on the lid of the toilet while Megan showered.

He waited a few minutes until he figured the worst of the cold was burned out of her by the hot water. "So what's wrong?"

He'd spoken quietly, but the way she stilled made it clear she'd heard him. She stayed frozen for a moment before she resumed running her hands through her hair under the water. "Nothing. What do you mean?"

He quirked an eyebrow, even though she wouldn't be able to see it through the foggy plastic of the shower stall. "You acted like you were pissed at Matt for laughing at you, but then you didn't seem pissed when you saw me. You seemed ... wary, like you were hiding something. So, what is it? What's wrong?"

She didn't freeze this time, but she still took her time answering. "Nothing. I'm just tired. It was a long day and then it was pouring when I left the tutoring center. I had to walk all the way across campus in that and I got really wet. It was just a sucky end to a sucky day."

He nodded. "That makes sense." She didn't respond. "Why was today so sucky?"

She stilled again. Not as long as before, but he still caught it. "No particular reason. Just one of those days, y'know?"

Her voice was falsely bright. He didn't buy that for a second. "Did that Isaac asshole get in your face again or something?"

"What? No." She laughed a little. "Nothing like that." Her answer sounded genuine. She was surprised that he'd asked. And she hadn't frozen like he'd touched a nerve like earlier. That seemed like the truth at least.

"Good. You know you can tell me if he bothers you again, right?"

She laughed again, warmer this time. "I know. You and Matt will beat the shit out of him for me." He could see her head shaking, her features indistinct, her dark hair and peach skin a blur through the plastic.

He smiled. "That's right we will." He forced himself to relax when he realized he was involuntarily flexing his arms where they were crossed over his chest. It wasn't a bluff. He'd beat the shit out of anyone for Megan if they were bothering her. "So what happened?"

She shook her head again as she turned off the shower and opened the door. She grabbed a towel and wrapped it around herself over her breasts. Chris couldn't help being a little disappointed that she'd covered herself up already. "It's really nothing, Chris. I'm fine. It was just a crap day. I'm glad it's over."

He looked up from where her arms were still crossed over her breasts to her face. She had a soft smile on her lips and looked sincere. "Okay." He stood, reaching for her again, bringing her in against his chest and rubbing his hands over her back. "You know you can talk to me if you need to, right?" She nodded against his chest. "Good. Now, let's finish getting you dry and warm."

Chris tilted her head up and took her lips in a kiss. She responded right away, trying to control the kiss, but he wouldn't let her. He tugged at the towel, pulling it from around her, wrapping it over her shoulders and running his hands on her arms while he continued to kiss her. When he decided her arms were dry, he broke off the kiss and pulled the towel up to her hair. She giggled when he covered her head with the towel and rubbed her scalp. His hands looked huge compared to the size of her skull. He squished her hair through the towel, trying to blot out as much water as possible, then pulled the towel back far enough so that her face peeked out. She was trying to glare at him, but kept ruining it with laughter.

He smiled down at her and pulled her against him. Her breasts squished against his bare torso, nipples tightening, and he kissed her again. She wrapped her arms around his neck, and he ran the towel in his hands down to her ass. He gripped her through the fabric and lifted her up. She immediately wrapped her legs around him, clinging to his shoulders and hips. He carried her into the bedroom and they fell onto the bed together.

Sliding down her body, he found her pussy, first with his fingers, then with his mouth. He quickly brought her to orgasm before he shoved his jeans and boxers down and rolled on a condom. He'd been hard since she'd stripped before her shower and knew he wouldn't last long. She wrapped her arms and legs around him, bringing his face close to hers so she could kiss him again.

After reaching a shuddering climax, he collapsed on top of her, his jeans still around his thighs and his legs dangling off the bed. She cradled his head next to hers, stroking her hands through his hair, and he turned to kiss her shoulder and neck. She giggled and squirmed under him, then pushed at his shoulders. "That tickles, and you need to deal with the condom."

He grinned down at her, tickling her sides and kissing her once more before he got up to toss the condom in the bathroom trash can. When he came back out, Megan was pulling a long sleeved thermal t-shirt and a pair of lounge pants out of the dresser. He zipped and buttoned his pants while he watched her get dressed. "Warmer now?"

Her head full of damp curls popped out of the shirt and she smiled at him. "Much. Thank you."

He grinned back. "My pleasure. Anytime."

She laughed, and he retrieved a dry t-shirt for himself before they went out to join Matt for dinner.

"When are you leaving for Thanksgiving break?" Matt's voice drifted from the living room into the kitchen where Megan was doing dishes since Matt had made them all dinner. Chris would normally have helped, but he'd said he needed to do some research, so Megan shooed him away to do it herself.

Megan turned off the water in the sink and set the plate in her hand in the dishwasher without clinking it against the other dishes so she could hear Chris's answer to Matt's question. Her recent conversation with Charlie burned in her mind. In moments she would know the answer to her question about whether Chris intended to ask her to go with him. This was the perfect opportunity to ask. She held her breath and waited for his answer.

"Probably early Wednesday afternoon. You wanna ride together again?"

Megan crinkled her eyebrows together. She knew they were both from Western Washington, but she didn't think their parents lived close enough together for them to carpool. Had they known each other before coming to school here? She didn't think so, but hearing them talk made her realize that she didn't know all that much about either of them.

She heard the sound of fabric rustling, one of them shifting in his seat, before Matt answered. "Yeah, sure. My sister's going to be home, and I doubt my mom will want either of us going anywhere for the few days we'll all be there. Drop me off. If I get desperate I'll text you to come get me on Friday. When are you planning on heading home?"

"Saturday, probably. Abby and I were talking about us all getting together that weekend. She thinks she misses us after spending all that time here over the summer."

The smile in Chris's voice was unmistakable, his affection for Abby clear. Megan felt it like a punch to the gut. When had Abby made plans with Chris? Why didn't Megan know? Was she not invited? That ... hurt. It felt like betrayal, both from her best friend and her ... whatever Chris was to her. The word *boyfriend* rattled around in her head, but she couldn't bring herself to label him as that, not even to herself. Not after that sucker punch. He had to know that she'd be able to hear them. The walls were thin and there wasn't even a door between the kitchen and the living room. So, no invite home with him. Not much of a boyfriend.

She sucked in a breath, blinking hard a few times, and turned the water back on to finish with the dishes.

Apparently she'd be on her own for Thanksgiving break. On her own to defend herself against her parents and on her own while the people she was closest to hung out without her.

Fan-fucking-tastic.

Chris patted the seat next to him and moved his arm to the back of the couch so that Megan could sit down. He sat with his bare feet up on the coffee table crossed at the ankle and his laptop balanced on his thighs. Megan settled in next to him where he'd indicated, and he wrapped his arm around her, pulling her in close, shooting her a quizzical look when she resisted at first. She didn't respond, but shifted so her feet were on the couch and she leaned back against him with his arm across her chest. They sat like this often while doing homework or watching TV.

Megan glanced over at his computer screen. "I thought you said you were doing research."

"I am."

She turned her head so she could look at his face and arched an eyebrow. "And what class is that for?"

He grinned down at her. "I just said research. I never said it was for a class."

She grunted in response and turned back to look at the screen again. "Fine. What are you researching?"

"Regional Combines."

"Regional what now?"

"Combines." He couldn't help laughing a little at the confusion on her face. It wasn't very often that he knew more about something than she did. He was going to enjoy this moment for as long as he could.

"Combines," she repeated. "Like one of those big tractor things?"

He laughed at that. Her lips were pursed in frustration and he couldn't help kissing her to try to smooth the irritation off of her face. She remained stiff, not kissing him back, and looked just as cranky with him when he drew back. He chuckled again. "No, not farm equipment. Regional Combines are basically tryouts for the NFL."

"Oh." Her face cleared for a moment before a mixture of curiosity and confusion took over. "When are they?"

"Most of them are in February. There's one in Arizona that's still open for registration. I'll probably go there."

He took a deep breath and clicked on the button to register. He could feel Megan's eyes on him, but he didn't look at her.

"How does it work?"

He spared her a quick glance, noting the corners of her mouth pulled down in a frown and the crinkle between her brows. "Well, I go and participate in the Regional Combine. If they like me enough, I get invited to the Super Regional in March, and from there I could get picked up in the draft." He drew in a deep breath and blew it out, clicking through and filling out the registration form, leaning over to pull his wallet out of his back pocket so he could pay the fee. Megan watched him the whole time, and when he looked up, Matt had paused his video game and was watching him from where he sat in the recliner. He lifted his chin at Matt. "Wanna go with me?"

Matt studied him for a minute before shaking his head. "Nah, man. I'm good. College ball's been fun, but I don't really want to go pro."

Chris shrugged and turned back to the computer. He'd finished registering, so he really didn't need to do anything, but he clicked around on the website anyway, not sure what Megan's reaction would be. She shifted next to him and sat up. He let his arm fall away from her, and she situated herself so she sat cross-legged on the middle couch cushion, looking at him, and he finally shut the laptop and gave her his attention.

"What are your chances?"

Chris flinched a little, surprised. That wasn't what he'd expected. He shrugged. "I don't know. Probably not great. But it's my only shot." He looked away from her, running a hand through his hair and rubbing the back of his neck. "I've wanted to go pro since I was a little kid. I'm eligible for the combines this year. If I don't try, I think I'll always regret it." He lifted his eyes to hers again, a crooked smile on his face. He wanted to plead with her for her support, or at least her understanding, but couldn't do that. So, he pasted on a smile in anticipation of her criticism.

Instead she studied him, her brown eyes serious, her face impassive. Finally, she nodded once, whether in acknowledgment or agreement, he wasn't sure. "Are you still planning on graduating in May?"

"Yeah." Leave it to Megan to care more about school.

"Then go get your books. You've got homework." She shoved at his shoulder, and he laughed at her feeble attempt to move him. But he got up, took the computer back to the bedroom, and got what he needed to get through before the next day. He was doing better than he'd ever expected in his classes, especially since he'd kind of given up before the semester had even started. Megan had gotten him to focus more on his classes. Since she wouldn't budge on her own study time, it was easier to just study with her and get it over with. Then he could get to more enjoyable activities with Megan.

Chapter Seventeen

A collective groan went up from the crowd. The Marycliff University football team had just had the ball stripped with less than two minutes left in the fourth quarter. It had been raining most of the game, and the field was muddy, making everything slippery and easy for the other team to force the running back to fumble. They were down by three, and this latest turnover meant they were unlikely to get another chance to score unless they managed a last minute interception and touchdown. A disappointing way to end the season, especially with their final game at home.

Next to Megan, Abby sat down to start packing up her things. Lance still stood, bouncing on his toes, as though he could change the outcome of the game through the force of his will. Megan smiled at the thought, and turned her attention back to the game. The other team was only making running plays, not allowing any interceptions. The MU defense did a good job of holding them, not letting them gain much yardage, but they couldn't force a turnover. The clock ran down, and MU lost, the sense of defeat as oppressive as the heavy clouds overhead.

The MU players shook hands on the field with the other team before they headed back to the locker room, leaving the winning players to celebrate on the field until their coaches shooed them off.

"Well, that's a bummer." Abby stood back up, folded their stadium blanket, and shoved it into her bag.

Megan nodded. "Yeah. The guys'll be disappointed."

"You think they'll still want to go to a party tonight?"

Lance snorted on Abby's other side. "More than ever, probably. That's a sucky way to end their last season. They'll both want to drink." He shifted his gaze to Megan. "Did you drive tonight? You should plan on being DD for them unless you guys all want to cram in with us."

Megan chuckled. "No thanks. I know neither of them like riding in the back of either of your cars. I was planning on driving anyway. I figured if they won, they'd want to celebrate and if they lost, they'd want to drown their sorrows. Either way, they deserve not to drive tonight."

Lance nodded and took the bag from Abby before they headed down the stairs.

Megan tugged at Abby's sleeve to get her attention. "I'm going to stop at the concessions and get a hot chocolate. I'm freezing after standing out here in the cold rain."

"Good idea. I'll come with you."

Abby told Lance, who nodded and kissed her. "I'll meet you guys at the usual place."

They split off from Lance once they were inside and headed to the coffee stand. Abby tugged Megan into the bathroom on the way there. "Better pee now while we have the chance!"

Megan grinned and followed her in.

Abby watched Megan in the mirror while they washed their hands, waiting for the restroom to empty before she spoke. "So, how are things going? I haven't heard from you much lately, and you seem to avoid answering questions."

Megan groaned. "Now, Abby? You want to talk about this now?"

Abby shrugged. "Like I said, you dodge my questions on the phone and over text. I have you trapped now, and we still have to wait for Chris and Matt to come out. As covered in mud as they got, I'm sure they'll take longer than normal." She reached for a paper towel and leaned her hip against the sink while she dried her hands. "Out with it. I know something's going on with you. What's up?"

Megan reached for a paper towel of her own, avoiding Abby's probing gaze, deciding what and how much to tell her. Finally she blurted out, "I'm falling for Chris and I don't think he feels the same way about me."

Abby froze, her mouth hanging open. After what felt like a hundred years, but was probably more like ten seconds, she closed her mouth with a snap. "Wow. That's not what I thought you were going to say at all. I'm happy for you, but concerned about the fact that you don't think Chris feels the same way. Any particular reason why?"

Megan shrugged and turned away to toss her paper towel in the trashcan. She took a deep breath. "At the Halloween party I saw some chick trying to make a move on him. I'm pretty sure he turned her down."

"The slutty devil girl?" At Megan's nod, Abby continued. "Yeah, I saw that too. He definitely turned her down. I think he tried to be nice, but she was pretty persistent, and not at all happy to get rejected if the look on her face was anything to go by."

Megan nodded again. "Thanks. That's good to know."

"Was that it? Feel better now?"

Megan shook her head. "No. While I was watching them—and I do appreciate you clearing that up, because I didn't see all of that from where I was standing. Anyway, some other chick dressed as a Playboy bunny—" Abby snorted at that, and Megan broke off, a grin on her face. "I know, right? Anyway, she came up and started telling me how Chris doesn't do relationships and he was only with me because we live in the same house, and it was just a matter of time before he got bored and moved on, especially once the season ended." Abby took a breath to say something, but Megan kept going without letting her talk. "And then Charlie called me trying to convince me to go home for Thanksgiving and I was hoping that Chris might ask me to go home with him, but that night when he and Matt were talking, it seemed like the thought of asking me never even crossed his mind."

Megan let out a breath and shook her head. "It's just a big mess, and I don't know what to think or who to believe."

Abby leveled a look at her. "Okay, first things first. Have you talked to him about any of this?"

Megan looked down at her hands, fiddling with the ring she wore on her thumb, and shook her head. "No."

"Okay, well, you can't expect the guy to know what's going on with you if you don't talk to him. You said yourself that you know he hasn't ever had a girlfriend, at least not in college."

"So?"

Abby raised her eyebrows. "So? Chris is a nice guy when he wants to be, but he's clueless about members of the opposite sex."

Megan snorted. "Are you kidding? Have you seen him flirt?"

A grin split Abby's face. "Yes, and that's not what I'm talking about. Sure, he knows how to flirt, but he doesn't know anything about sustained relationships. I seriously doubt that he left you out of his Thanksgiving plans on purpose." Abby paused for a moment, playing with her lower lip for a second. "He's different with you. I know I haven't known him for much longer than you have, but you've only known him since you moved in, really. He doesn't act the same since you guys got together."

Megan took that in without saying anything.

Abby stepped closer and rubbed Megan's back. "Just don't read too much into anything without talking to him, okay? And don't believe what some skank dressed like a Playboy bunny says to you at a party. Those jersey chasers can get jealous and catty. You should've figured that out by now."

"Yeah, okay." Megan blew out a breath and forced herself to smile. "Can we get out of here and get our hot chocolate now? We can talk about this later when we're not in a stadium bathroom, okay?"

Abby laughed. "Okay. If you decide you can't handle going home for Thanksgiving you can come hang out with Lance and me. Either way, you should come over during the break since you'll be alone. We can watch movies and hang out like we used to."

Megan hooked her arm with Abby's as they walked to the coffee cart. "Sounds good. Thanks, Abs."

Abby squeezed Megan's arm. "Anytime."

Walking out of the locker room to find Megan, Lance, and Abby waiting for him and Matt at their usual meeting spot eased the knot of tension that still twisted in his gut. Wrapping his arms around Megan and having her meet him partway for a kiss soothed the frustration and disappointment still zinging through his veins. She tasted like chocolate, and he didn't want to break the kiss, but the others were waiting, so he pulled back. He couldn't help dropping one more little kiss on her mouth and nuzzling her hair, breathing her in.

His last game and they fucking lost. He swung between bitter disappointment at ending his football career this way, and wild hope that maybe it wasn't all over. Maybe he'd do well at the Regional Combines and make it all the way to the NFL draft. He didn't care if he didn't get picked up until the last round. Of course, earlier would be nice, but since he wasn't being courted by scouts, realistically, his chances were pretty low for getting that far at all.

Megan's presence steadied out those emotions and brought him back down. A few drinks at a party to commiserate with his teammates, then getting home to bury himself inside her would make him feel much better. He was tempted to skip the party altogether. They could have a few beers at home and he could get her naked that much sooner. But he'd already promised his teammates he'd come out. This was their last post-game party. Their last night as a team. He couldn't bring himself to bail completely.

Lance lifted his chin at Chris when he looked up. "Ready?"

Chris glanced at Matt who raised his eyebrows, then down at Megan. She grinned. "I'm driving. You guys can safely drown your sorrows, and I'll take you both home and put you to bed."

Chris laughed. "Babe, I better be the only one you're taking to bed."

Megan smacked his chest and stuck her tongue out at him. "I'm not going to leave Matt on the floor or stumbling his way to bed and breaking something. But I'm not going to climb in with him, either."

"Fine, whatever. Just so long as you end up in bed with me, I don't really care."

Megan smirked at him but didn't say anything, and they all headed out to the parking lot. The rain had finally let up some time during the fourth quarter, and hadn't started again, even though the clouds remained, a gloomy ceiling making it prematurely dark outside. They dodged puddles on their way to their cars, keeping their heads down against the wind that had picked up.

The party was at Sullivan's place, not too far from campus. Chris always felt a little weird when he rode in Megan's car. He preferred to drive but was grateful she'd volunteered to be DD. He didn't know if he'd get that drunk tonight, though, still just wanting to get home and spend time with Megan. Maybe they could foist Matt off on Abby and Lance again. That way they could leave early if Matt wasn't ready to go yet.

He sat in the back being his usual calm self, but Chris knew that he was pissed about the way the game had ended. Matt had tried to strip the ball during those last minutes of the game, and almost managed to do it. The running back had bobbled the ball, but had managed to bring it in before Matt could tip it again and bat it away.

The party was well underway by the time they got there. Sullivan must've had people there to get things started before the game even ended. They had to park a couple of blocks away, which just cemented Chris's plans to only have a few drinks and head home. He didn't want to make Megan get his and Matt's drunk asses all the way to the car in the cold when she was parked that far away.

A round of cheers greeted their entrance, and they grabbed their drinks before settling on the couch in the living room, him in the corner with Megan on his lap and Matt next to them. Lance and Abby walked in just as they were getting settled, and they kicked a sophomore off the couch to make room for them. They spent time drinking and dissecting the game and what went wrong, bemoaning the end of the season, the seniors talking about their plans for next semester or after graduation. Someone got out a bottle of tequila, lime quarters, and a salt shaker and they took turns doing shots.

After a few rounds, one of the guys called out, "Let's do body shots!" A girl squealed, whether in anticipation or not Chris wasn't sure.

He grinned at Megan, who laughed and pulled her shirt to one side, exposing more of her shoulder for him, handed him the salt shaker, and put a lime wedge in her mouth. His grin grew wider, and he leaned forward, licking and sucking where her shoulder met her neck. He sprinkled the salt on the wet spot he'd just made, taking the shot from the redhead who was doling them out. He licked the salt, knocked back the tequila, and sucked the lime out of Megan's mouth. He spat it to the side before taking her mouth again, kissing her deeply. A round of cheers went up around them, and Megan pulled back, laughing.

She leaned forward to talk in his ear so she could be heard without shouting. "I'm going to go use the bathroom and get something to drink."

He watched her ass as she picked her way through the crowd until she rounded the corner and he couldn't see her anymore. Laying his head against the back of the couch, he closed his eyes for a moment, the adrenaline from the game long since burned out of his muscles, and the alcohol making him pleasantly tired.

After what seemed like just a moment, he felt someone climb onto his lap, straddling him. Soft hands gripped his cheeks, then lips were on his. A tongue forced its way into his mouth.

This was wrong. She was taller, heavier, and tasted like liquor instead of soda. He couldn't pull his head back because he was trapped against the back of the couch. His eyes popped open, but he could only make out a halo of red hair.

Who the hell was this chick? He gripped her hips and tried to push her away. She seemed to take it as encouragement and ground her pelvis into his lap. He got his hands up to her wrists and managed to push her back enough to break the kiss.

The redhead that had handed him the shot stared down into his face, smiling. She looked vaguely familiar, but he couldn't place her.

Rage worked its way past the alcohol. "What the fuck?"

The smile on her face slipped, but she tried to reach for him again. He pushed her backward and stood up, letting her fall to the ground.

Shock and anger took over her face, her features pinching together. "What the fuck, Chris?" She scrambled up off the floor and pulled her dress down.

"That's what I want to know! What the fuck? Who the hell are you and why are you climbing in my lap and kissing me?" He towered over her, yelling, causing her to back away from him. Hands on his arms started pulling at him, but he shrugged them off, crossing his arms and waiting for her to answer. "Well?"

She looked around, trying to find support. "You were interested in me at the pool party. We kissed. You acted like you wanted to hook up, but then you got busy and I wanted to pick up where we left off."

"And watching me make out with someone else made you think tonight was the night to make your move?"

Her eyes flicked over Chris's shoulders, then she put her shoulders back and firmed her sneer. "Aren't you done with that bitch yet? You've been fucking her for months. Everyone knows it's time for you to move on."

Chris's mouth fell open, and he drew a deep breath, prepared to tell her exactly what she needed to know, but Matt's voice in his ear stopped him. "Dude. I know. But Megan just left. She was on her way back and saw that bitch trying to shove her tongue down your throat. She turned around right before you dumped her on the floor. I just heard the door slam. She's gone. You need to go after her. Now."

Chris closed his mouth and nodded once, not sure what to do. He was too buzzed to try to drive. Maybe he could catch her before she got to the car. God, he hoped so.

Chapter Eighteen

Megan froze. There was some chick on Chris's lap, kissing him. He had his hands on her hips and wasn't protesting. She swallowed against the lump in her throat, fighting to keep down the contents of her stomach that threatened to make a reappearance. Everything she'd feared unfolded right in front of her eyes. It was like talking to Abby about it tonight had put it all out there, and here was the proof she'd been wanting.

Wow. It hadn't taken him long to move on. She'd been gone for less than ten minutes. The shots might've gone to his head, but she'd figured he was able to hold his liquor better than this unless he were interested.

She blinked hard to try to dispel the burning sensation in her eyes. Someone bumped into her, jostling her out of her frozen state. "Sorry," they muttered before moving on.

Megan whirled and made her way back to the kitchen and the alcohol. She stopped in the doorway. Shit. She was driving. She couldn't get trashed right now no matter how much she wanted to. Fuck.

Pushing her way back to the front door, she ignored the sounds of annoyance from the people she moved out of her way or slipped between. She could only focus on getting out the door. Once she got to her car she could figure the rest out.

She paused on the front step. The cold air hit her like a slap in the face. That was what brought tears to her eyes. The cold. And the wind. That was all. She took a deep, shuddery breath and wrapped her arms around herself. Head down, she started the trek to her car. The temperature had dropped as the wind had picked up. She guessed it was close to freezing now, the sparkling moisture on the sidewalk hinting at either thick frost or ice by morning.

Footsteps pounded behind her, and she moved to the right so whoever was running could pass her easily. A hand grabbed her left bicep, stopping her and turning her around.

Chris stood in front of her, breathing hard. She ripped her arm away from him. "What do you want?"

"Where are you going?"

She stared at him for a moment, not even sure how to respond to that. "I'm leaving."

"Why?"

An ugly laugh escaped her chest before she could throttle it. It was bad enough that he would know he affected her enough for her to bail like this, but she couldn't handle having him see all of her emotions. It was too raw. Too real. And he didn't deserve that knowledge. She needed to put on her cold bitch face and get away before she couldn't hold it together anymore. "It looked like you had your hands full enough. You don't seem to need me anymore."

He ran a hand through his hair and over his face, a gesture of frustration that she recognized. It also meant he didn't know what to say or do. Fan-fucking-tastic. He didn't even know how to defend himself. The simplest defense being that she attacked him or something. Not that that was likely judging by what she'd seen. Or that he wasn't into it, even if that bitch had climbed onto him uninvited. "Fuck, Megan. I don't know what you saw, but I promise it wasn't what it looked like."

Another bark of laughter came out, this one more incredulous. "That's rich, Chris. So there wasn't a redhead in your lap with her tongue down your throat? I just imagined that?" She snorted and turned to head for the car.

His hand fell on her shoulder, but she shrugged him off, not even looking back. "Megan. Listen! Wait a goddamn minute and let me tell you what happened!"

She cast a look over her shoulder, but didn't stop. Chris was keeping pace beside her. "You know what? It doesn't even matter. It's not like this could ever go anywhere anyway. We both know this was just about convenience. If you're ready to move on to another fuck buddy, or a series of hookups like you used to do, that's your business. The season's over, so you'll have more time for that kind of shit anyway, right? I just don't want to watch, that's all."

She put her head down and started to walk faster. It wasn't like Chris wouldn't be able to keep up. Even buzzed he could outrun her any day. He was in good shape and his legs were longer than hers. But she hoped he'd get the point that she was done with this conversation, done with him, and to leave her alone.

He followed her as far as her car, stopping on the sidewalk by the passenger door while she went around the car to the driver's side. She looked at him over the roof of the car. His face was twisted like he was in pain and goosebumps danced over the bare skin of his arms.

"Fuck, Megan. Please? Just listen. You don't have to talk, just listen. Please."

She shook her head, not trusting her voice to speak without breaking. Her hands were remarkably steady when she shoved the key in the ignition. She slammed the car into drive and pulled away from the curb without even bothering to signal. Fortunately no cars were coming.

On the way back to the house she realized that she was so screwed. She and Chris shared a room. All their stuff was intermingled. Even if he had his own room still, what was she going to do? She couldn't stay in that house, couldn't handle seeing him. What if he brought some chick home?

She pulled over on the side of the road, not entirely sure where she was. In her anger and hurt, she'd just been driving, not paying attention to where she was going. She pulled out her phone and sent a text to Abby. Maybe she could crash there while she figured shit out. At least the semester would be over soon. Finding a roommate would be easier between semesters. Not as good as at the beginning or end of summer, but better than mid-semester.

Come back to the party. I'll meet you out front and give you my key.

Megan let out a breath at the text in her hand. She was a little nervous about going back to the party. What if Chris tried to talk to her again? She couldn't handle that right now. It was only through years of practice from dealing with her parents that she was able to keep the rage and tears in check. But her tenuous hold on her emotions wouldn't last much longer. She needed to get her things and get to Abby's house before she let it out. She couldn't even let out a little of her frustration for fear that everything would come out before she was somewhere safe.

Okay. Be there in 5. Don't tell anyone.

I have to tell Lance you'll be at our apartment tonight. But I won't tell him I'm handing off my key until you're gone.

Good enough. Thanks.

Paying more attention and using her blinker this time, Megan turned around and headed back to the party. She pulled up in front of the house where Abby stood shivering in her long sleeved t-shirt, arms crossed and shoulders hunched, wisps of blonde hair that had come free from her ponytail whipping in the wind. Megan rolled down the window and Abby thrust the key into her hand, leaned in, and hugged her.

"Thanks again, Abs."

"Anytime. I'll make sure the guys get home. You'll have to crash on the couch. See you when Lance and I get home."

"Right. Thanks. See you there."

Abby waved before she turned and ran back to the door, in a hurry to get out of the cold. Megan left again, paying more attention to where she was going this time. Her first stop was at the house to pack some essentials. She wasn't sure how long she'd be at Abby and Lance's house, but figured she could come back for more once things were sorted out, so she threw her toiletries, makeup, pjs and a change of clothes in her backpack. At the last second she grabbed a sketch pad and her pastels and stuffed them in before she grabbed her phone charger and headed for Lance and Abby's. She hoped Lance kept the fridge stocked with beer. She planned on drinking whatever she could find and paying them back for it later.

"Megan!" Chris pushed the front door shut, barely managing not to slam it. He flexed his hands at his sides while he waited for an answer that didn't come. The house was quiet, the lights all off. The door to their bedroom was cracked, no telltale spill of light flooding out. He ran his hands through his hair, clutched it in his hands and pulled, trying to use the sting of pain on his scalp to help him focus, to figure out what to do.

He pushed the door open and held his breath, hoping to find her curled on the bed, or the door to the bathroom closed, indicating she might be in there. But the room was still, no signs of life anywhere. The bed looked the same as it had when he'd left earlier, the blankets a little rumpled, but no sign anyone had been in it in the last few hours. Megan's things were all still there, no sign of hurried packing and leaving. He let out his breath, relieved at that. She just hadn't come home yet, maybe.

After Megan had left, he'd gone back inside, drained a cup of beer, then thought better of getting raging drunk. He needed to talk to Megan, and he needed to be sober, or mostly sober, to do that. He'd found Abby and argued with her for ten or fifteen minutes to convince her to take him home. Matt and Lance had just sat there watching them argue. Finally, she'd given in. Maybe Megan was somewhere else, blowing off some steam before she came home and had to confront him. He nodded to himself. Yeah. That was probably what was going on.

Chris flipped on the light in the bathroom. He needed to pee before he sat on the couch with a bottle of Gatorade to wait for her. The relief that had just settled in his chest coalesced and turned to ice, dropping low in his belly. There was too much space on the little bathroom counter. Megan's bag of makeup and the lotions she kept next to it were gone. He yanked open the door to the shower stall and noted the absence of her shampoo, conditioner, and razor.

She'd already been home and left. Going back into the bedroom, he noticed that her backpack wasn't in its usual spot and her phone charger wasn't plugged in next to the bed either. A cursory glance at the closet told him that she hadn't taken much with her, but it was clear that she wouldn't be back tonight.

Chris turned and punched the doorframe. "Fuck!"

It was obvious now that Abby had argued with him to give Megan time to get in and out of the house before he could get home. Why hadn't he seen that before? He had thought he'd worn her down with his stubbornness, but she had capitulated too easily when it came down to it.

"Motherfucker." He kept up a steady stream of muttered curses while he grabbed the Gatorade out of the fridge, whatever buzz he'd managed to achieve at the party long since gone. This whole day had been a huge clusterfuck. And he wasn't sure how to fix any of it.

He pulled out his phone and texted Megan. *Where are you? We need to talk.*

He stared at it, willing her to text him back. Setting the phone on the kitchen counter so he wouldn't chuck it across the room in his frustration, he took a few deep breaths and chugged the sports drink. When he was done, he still hadn't gotten a response. He threw the empty bottle at the door to the side yard instead of his phone. It didn't help.

Abby. She had to know where Megan was. *Where's Megan?*

He tapped his fingers on the edge of his phone while he waited for her to answer. Surely she wouldn't just ignore him. After what felt like an eternity, but was really more like two minutes, his message showed that it had been read and the three little dots were flashing to indicate that she was typing. Final-fucking-ly. Maybe now he'd get some kind of answer.

Megan needs some space right now.

No she doesn't. She needs to talk to me.

The pause this time was longer. But Abby texted back. *She saw you kissing another chick. Who was sitting on your lap. I'm not sure what there is for you to talk about.*

That's not what happened. You were there, tell her what went down and then have her call me.

I was in the bathroom. All I know is what I was told. Megan saw you kissing someone else.

Fuck fuck fuck. Could he not catch a break? If Abby had witnessed what happened, then this misunderstanding would be over already. Matt or Lance had to have seen that chick climb on him and maul his face and then him toss her on the floor. That room was full of people. He had to be able to get someone to tell her what really happened, even if she wouldn't listen to him.

Is she at your place?

He was already grabbing his keys and heading out the door when her response came in.

Give her some space. You can try to talk tomorrow.

Fuck that. He was going to explain himself if he had to bust down the door. Lance would understand. Lance had to be on his side.

The drive to Lance and Abby's apartment seemed to take far longer than normal. The lights were all red, and he kept getting stuck behind the slowest people in town. He needed to talk to Megan. Now. Waiting like this was torture.

He slammed the car in park in the closest spot to their door he could find. The rain stung his bare arms. He'd left his jacket somewhere, and he couldn't even remember where.

His fist hammered the door. "Megan! We need to talk!" He pounded again.

After beating on the door yet again, it swung open and Lance filled the space. Chris tried to muscle past him, but Lance's hands on his chest pushed him back and held him outside the door. Chris pushed against him, trying to see over his shoulder into the apartment, but he couldn't see anyone inside.

"Whoa, Chris. Back up. I said back up!"

Lance shoved him, and Chris stumbled back a couple steps. Lance took advantage of the space and stepped outside, pulling the door closed behind him. Chris had been hoping that Lance had gotten softer since he wasn't playing anymore and Chris was just coming off a season full of hard workouts and harder practices. No such luck. Lance still lifted regularly from the looks of it.

He really didn't want to punch one of his best friends, but if Lance wasn't going to move out of his way soon, he just might. Why was Lance coming between him and Megan?

Chris ran a hand through his hair. "Is Megan here? I know she's gotta be here. I need to talk to her."

Lance leaned back against the door, his arms crossed, blocking the handle, his eyes on Chris's torso, reading his movements, ready to defend the door more if necessary. Lance's eyes flicked to Chris's face for a moment. "Look, man. I know you want to talk to Megan, but I don't think now's a good time."

"What the fuck, man? You were there, right? You saw what happened. I didn't do anything." Chris could feel himself losing his grip on the situation. He took a step closer to Lance so that they were only inches apart. Too bad he and Lance were the same height. His chances at physical intimidation were low, but he'd pull whatever tricks he had in his arsenal, small as that may be. "You need to let me in. I need to talk to Megan, explain what happened."

Lance's hand came up, stopping him. "Dude, you need to take a step back. I'm on your side here. I know what happened."

Chris deflated. Someone was on his side. He took a step back and put a few more inches between him and Lance. "Good. Okay. Then let me talk to Megan." He gestured toward the door.

Lance shook his head, and Chris had to force his hands to relax so they weren't forming fists. "I already told you. Now's not the time to talk to her." He looked away, toward the street lamp in the parking lot, watching the rain falling outside the protective cover of the doorway, then back at Chris. "I'm sorry, man. I already tried talking to her, but she's not in a place where she's willing to listen. Give her some time to calm down. Try again tomorrow."

Chris took another step back, turning around and threading his fingers in his own hair. "Fuck." He said it quietly, then again, louder. "Fuck!"

"I know. I'm sorry, man. If I thought she'd see you without throwing things at your head or clawing your eyes out, I'd let you in. Let her cool down. I'll see if I can talk to her tonight and explain what happened. If I can, I'll try to get her to call you."

Chris turned back around, and he could see the frustration written on Lance's face. He let out a breath, and nodded. "Thanks, man. I appreciate it."

Lance looked him up and down and shrugged. "I'll do what I can. I'm not promising anything, though."

Chris nodded again, feeling dejected now. Lance stood up away from the door, one hand on the handle. "Night, man."

"Night." Chris turned and headed back out into the rain, walking slowly to his car. He didn't even notice the rain soaking through his shirt or the goosebumps where the cold water hit his skin. Once back in the car he sat there for a moment but didn't turn it on yet. He pounded a fist on the steering wheel. "Fuck!" He did it again. It didn't matter, though. Hitting things wouldn't ease the ache in his chest or unfreeze the ball in his gut. The only thing that could do that was talking to Megan and getting her to understand what had happened so she'd come home and curl up in his bed again.

Chapter Nineteen

Megan woke up disoriented and took a minute to come back to herself. She moved her head to look around the room and realized she wasn't home. Her fingers ran over the nubby texture of the upholstery while she lay on the couch facing the back trying to remain in her emotionless cocoon as long as possible.

They'd gotten lucky when they'd found this couch on Craigslist. It was in great shape, not too expensive, and a nice sage green. Most of the stuff in their budget had been 90s pastel clown barf colors, but they'd scored a sweet deal on this one. Megan let out a sigh, missing her old couch, missing living with Abby, missing the time before everything blew up in her face.

She rubbed the grit out of her swollen eyes, not looking forward to seeing her reflection in the mirror after having cried herself to sleep the night before. Lance and Abby's fridge had only held two beers, which she'd drained before they'd gotten home. She'd hoped to numb herself but knew it wouldn't be enough. At least she didn't have a hangover to add to her misery, much as she'd wanted to get drunk. Her current headache was all leftover from crying so much last night.

After she'd gotten to Lance and Abby's apartment she'd tossed her bag in a corner and gone straight for the fridge. They'd come home less than an hour later. Chris had texted her about the same time. She'd glanced at it and turned off her phone.

When he'd texted Abby, she'd looked at Megan. "He'll come over if someone doesn't answer him."

Megan had just nodded and gone to the bathroom while Abby texted him back. When he'd shown up after that, Megan and Abby had gone to the bedroom and waited for Lance to deal with him and send him away. Lance had tried to talk to her, to explain what had happened, but she'd shut him down. Abby knew

Megan well enough to convince him to leave her alone, give her some space, and they'd gone to their bedroom, casting glances at her as they went.

It wasn't until she was alone that Megan had let her tight rein on her emotions loose and the tears had started to fall. She'd muffled her sobs in the pillow until she'd exhausted herself and fallen asleep.

She heard doors opening and closing and the sounds of someone in the bathroom. Keeping her face to the couch, she tried to ignore the footsteps entering the living room, hoping they'd continue to the kitchen for breakfast or something and leave her alone for a little while longer. No such luck.

"Megan." It was Lance. "Can we talk?"

She deliberated for a moment. It had to happen sooner or later. She couldn't pull the blanket over her head and stay that way forever. Might as well get it over with. She rolled over to face Lance. He sat on the coffee table wearing a pair of blue flannel lounge pants and a worn looking white t-shirt, his arms resting on his knees.

Megan twisted her mouth into something she hoped resembled a smile. "You got the short straw, huh?"

He raised his eyebrows. "Abby's still sleeping." One corner of his mouth turned up. "She probably wouldn't want me talking to you without her, but ..."

He shrugged a shoulder. "You need to know what happened last night. Abby wasn't in there. But I was. And Matt was."

Megan rubbed her hands over her face and pressed the heels of her palms to her eyes for a moment before she sat up. "I don't know what you can say to make me feel any different. Chris had some chick on his lap and was kissing her. Since you were there, you obviously saw that."

Lance nodded. "Yeah. But you didn't see what happened before that and you left before you saw what happened next. Chris was sitting on the couch with his eyes closed. I think he might've even fallen asleep. That chick climbed onto his lap and started kissing him before he could react at all. He pushed her away and told her off. In front of everyone. If you'd stuck around for another thirty seconds, you would've seen it too."

The room started to get blurry, and Megan blinked hard a couple times and rubbed her eyes again to dispel the gathering moisture. She picked at some fuzz on the blanket, unable to meet Lance's eyes. "It doesn't really matter, Lance. She was grinding on him, and he didn't look too upset when I saw them. Even if he pushed her away after that. So he didn't take her in a room and fuck her then and there. It's just a matter of time. If not her, then it'll be someone else. I'm not going to wait around until our convenient arrangement isn't interesting enough and he starts to look elsewhere."

She could feel Lance's eyes on her, but she still wouldn't look up. He was silent for a long moment. "Maybe you're right," he said finally. That surprised her enough to look at him. He shook his head, a tiny motion. "I don't think you are, though. If that were the case, he would've moved on a long time ago."

Megan waved a hand, dismissing Lance's comment. "He's been gone half the semester, and when he's home he's busy with practice and school. He hasn't had time to get bored yet. But the season's over, he'll be home all the time now. He'll get bored. It's just a matter of time. I can't—" She bit off the words, shutting her mouth, not wanting to give too much away. Not to Lance, especially. He might be living with her best friend, but he was still tight with Chris. She didn't need whatever she said getting back to him.

Lance looked her over, his gaze more perceptive than she'd ever given him credit for. "I've known Chris for a while now." She nodded. She knew they'd been friends since they were freshmen, along with Matt. "I haven't ever seen him with anyone more than once." He caught her eyes and held her gaze. "Ever."

Megan nodded again. That wasn't new information either, but Lance seemed to think it was significant. "All the more reason to view our ... relationship as what it is. An anomaly. It can't last."

He nodded, looking thoughtful, scratching under his jaw. "You know, some might've said the same thing about Abby and me. Chris and Matt made a similar argument over the summer."

She let out a huff of laughter. "You can't compare Chris and me to you and Abby. It's not the same at all."

"How so?" He wore a neutral expression, eyebrows raised, inviting elaboration.

She shook her head again. "You were in love with each other before you tried to move back to Texas. Even if neither one of you would admit it, it was plain to see for everyone else."

Lance let out a thoughtful hum, and she wasn't sure if he was agreeing or not.

"Chris and I have ... an arrangement more than a relationship. We live in the same house. It's convenient for us both. He doesn't have to go around chasing girls when there's one waiting for him. That's what I am to him. Convenient. Until he gets bored."

"Right." Lance's tone made it clear he didn't believe her. Not that it mattered. Maybe she didn't see Chris as a convenience, but it was painfully clear that he didn't see her as more than that.

"Whatever. At the beginning of all this I made it clear that he just needed to let me know when he wanted our arrangement to end so he could hook up with other chicks. I'm taking last night as his notice. I just don't want to listen to him fucking someone else in the next room, okay?" The last part came out a little more heated than she'd intended, but Lance didn't seem surprised or upset by her vehemence. Instead, he just nodded slowly, a knowing look on his face.

"Alright. Does that mean you're planning on moving out of the house?"

"Yeah. I can't—" She swallowed hard. "I can't stay there anymore."

He nodded. "Matt'll be disappointed. He hates finding roommates. But stay as long as you need. If you need help finding a new place or moving your stuff, let me know."

He stood, and Megan watched him, not quite sure how to respond. First he was defending Chris, trying to repair their relationship. But now he seemed to have accepted that she didn't want to repair anything, regardless of the circumstances of the kiss at the party. At least he wasn't mad about her staying in his apartment.

Lance stretched, his hands almost touching the ceiling, scratched his stomach, and stepped toward the kitchen. "Hungry? We have eggs or cereal, whichever you prefer."

Megan blinked a couple times and stared after him. She wasn't expecting such a sudden subject change. "Uh, sure. Eggs sound good."

For the first time since he'd been at Marycliff, Chris was glad that they had classes the first two days of Thanksgiving week. Most people skipped out early on Tuesday, but still went to class on Monday. He hoped Megan would follow that trend instead of going home and taking the whole week off.

She hadn't come back to the house all weekend, and now he stood outside the tutoring center and waited to see if she'd come for work. Matt had his usual appointment with her and he'd gone in to see if she was there. Chris lounged outside the door, the air crisp and leaves crunching under his feet, hoping to catch her on her way out.

If this didn't work, he wasn't sure what he'd do. He'd tried calling and texting her again on Sunday, but her phone had gone straight to voicemail and she'd never responded to his texts. Lance had told him to give her some space, so he was trying to, but he needed to see her, to talk to her, figure out what was going on in her mind and plead his case. The longer she went without talking to him, the more worried he became.

Chris straightened when the door opened and Matt walked out. Alone. The brief swell of hope in his chest died before it had fully formed.

Matt walked toward him, his mouth set in a grim line. "She didn't come in today."

"Fuck." Chris took a deep breath and forced himself to relax his clenched fists instead of punching the maple tree next to him. "Shit. I was really counting on her being here today."

"I know. She won't answer my calls either. Have you talked to Lance or Abby since Saturday?"

Chris shook his head. "I'm trying not to act like a psycho stalker."

Matt's mouth twisted in a half grin. "Dude, you're waiting for her outside where she works. How is that not stalking?"

"Shut up. I said I was trying, not that I was succeeding. It's killing me that she won't talk to me. What else am I supposed to do?"

Matt sighed. "I know. I'm just messing with you. Let me call Lance and see if he knows what's going on. If he doesn't answer I'll try Abby. Lance knows what really happened. He has to have talked to her about it by now."

Chris nodded, waiting until Matt turned away and took a few steps before pressing his forehead against the bark of the tree, lightly banging his head against it a few times, trying to work out what to do.

Raucous laughter sounded from around the corner the building. Chris tried to ignore it, lost in the mire of his own frustration.

"No, dude, that's not how it went down." The voices grew louder. "He probably got tired of her, and who can blame him, y'know? Or she was whoring around with their other roommate and he didn't want to share. That's what happened with us."

"What? That's not what I heard, man." A new voice talked over the first one and a chorus of other voices made noises of disbelief and laughter. "I heard she never even gave it up to you, that you were chasing her all summer and couldn't hit that no matter what you tried."

More laughter, even louder, and the first guy's voice again. "What? No no no. That's not what happened at all. You guys saw Megan with me all summer. You know I wouldn't be hanging around with a chick if I weren't getting some on the regular. She can't give head to save her life, though." He made a chomping sound. "Gotta watch out for the teeth."

Chris's head snapped up and rage rolled through him at the sound of Megan's name. He turned to see a group of four guys coming around the corner, and he recognized the one in the lead. It was that asshole that had been giving her shit at the beginning of the semester. Isaiah? Ezra? Something like that. He was walking backward, looking back at his friends like they were an audience at a comedy club. That sophomore that he'd almost beaten the shit out of in the locker room was there too, laughing his ass off like this was the funniest conversation of the year.

Not waiting for the next response, Chris grabbed the lead asshole—Isaac, that was his name—spun him around, and pushed him against the brick wall. "You obviously haven't gotten the message that Megan is off limits as a subject of conversation."

The jackass laughed and pushed at Chris's hands where they clutched the fabric of his sweatshirt. "Look, dude. It's not a big deal. I'm sure we could swap some fun stories."

Chris slammed him into the wall. Not too hard, just enough so that his teeth snapped shut and he stopped laughing. "I don't think we can. See, from what I've heard, your boy over there's right. She wouldn't give you the time of day, and you were chasing after her all summer without getting anything more than a couple kisses. And that pissed you off, so you started spreading rumors all over campus about what a slut she is."

"That's not what happened. No, see, we—"

Chris slammed him into the wall again, a little harder. "You think I give a shit what you think happened? Let me be clear. I don't. I don't want to hear your version of events. I don't want to hear you talking about Megan Davidson ever again. Got it?"

Isaac let out a weak laugh, still trying to keep up his bravado and save face in front of his friends. "What's your problem, man? You're not even hitting that anymore. Everyone saw you with Brianna on your lap after the game Saturday."

Chris landed a punch to the gut and let go of Isaac so he could double over, his breath wheezing out with the impact. This asshole wasn't worth this much time and effort. It was time to make his point and figure out what to do about Megan. Chris grabbed Isaac's sweatshirt at the shoulder again, pulled him up a little, and bent down so their faces were close together. "Listen to me. I'm only going to say this once more. Leave Megan alone. Don't talk to her, don't talk about her. Pretend you never even met her, okay? If I hear you or your boys running your mouths about her again, you're going to get a lot worse than a fist in the gut."

"No, you listen, you fucker—"

Chris didn't let him continue, shutting him up with a punch to the jaw that knocked him on the ground. Shaking out his hand, Chris glared at the other guys standing around watching. One stepped back with his hands up, palms out, wanting no part in this exchange. The sophomore from the football team watched with wide eyes. He met Chris's gaze for a moment before he dropped his eyes and walked away.

Done with this, Chris turned and grabbed his bag. Matt came back around the other corner, his phone still in his hand, his eyes flicking from Chris to the guy on the ground behind him. He raised his eyebrows. "What happened here?"

Chris shook his head. "Tell you later. Did you talk to Lance or Abby?"

Matt's eyes flicked behind Chris once more, then fell in step beside him, letting that scene go. "Lance didn't answer. He's at work, so that's not surprising. I left him a voicemail. I did manage to talk to Abby."

"And?" Chris prodded when Matt didn't go on.

He sighed and shook his head. "You're not going to like what she had to say."

Chapter Twenty

"Your dad's carving the turkey and the rolls are in the oven. Once they're done it'll be time to eat."

Megan looked up from the football game she was watching with her brothers. "Okay, Mom. Do you need any help getting anything on the table?"

"Thanks, honey, but no. I've got it covered." Her mom gave her a small smile and a shake of her head, smoothing back a stray strand of blonde hair before she went back in the kitchen.

Megan's oldest brother Logan whacked her with a throw pillow from his seat on the other end of the couch. "What's up with you? Mom's acting weird. She's usually all over your offers of help, and today it seems like she's freezing you out."

Charlie, their other brother, turned to face them from where he lounged in a recliner, taking a drink of his soda, waiting for her answer. He took after their mother with his blond hair and blue eyes while Megan and Logan had their father's darker coloring. Megan grabbed the throw pillow out of Logan's grip and whacked him back.

"Hey! What was that for?"

"You started it." She tried to whack him again, but he snagged the pillow before she could hit him in the shoulder, then grabbed her wrist and pulled her closer to put her in a headlock. She squirmed and tried to get a hand up to the back of his head so she could pull his hair to get him to release her. He kept it pretty short, but there was enough to grab ahold of if she could get to it. But the way he had her pinned pushed her shoulder into the back of the couch, and she couldn't get her arm around. "Let me go!" She could hear Charlie cackling.

He held her without seeming to expend much effort. "Not until you answer my question."

Megan went limp, resigned. "Fine. Let me go and I'll answer your question."

He released her, and she sat up, running her hands through her hair, trying to straighten it. Dinner would be soon, and her mom wouldn't like it if she came to the table with her hair all messed up. She had enough problems with her parents without adding to it.

Blowing out a breath, she gestured at Charlie but kept her eyes on Logan. "Charlie over here told Mom and Dad that I have a boyfriend."

Charlie arched an eyebrow, but didn't say anything. Logan gestured for her to continue. "Oh, really? And do you?"

"No."

"That's not what it sounded like when we were talking on the phone a couple weeks ago." Charlie was still lounging back in his recliner, but his eyes were intense, focused on Megan. "I never took you for a liar, Megan."

Megan threw a pillow at Charlie. "I'm not lying. Now mind your own business, Charlie."

Logan cut Charlie off with a look when he opened his mouth to say something else, then turned to Megan. "Why does Charlie think you're lying about not having a boyfriend? Did you have a boyfriend earlier this month?"

Megan held his gaze for a moment, but couldn't maintain it while she shrugged and mumbled something so he couldn't hear. She couldn't bring herself to say yes, because was Chris ever really her boyfriend? But she couldn't say no either, because they had been in some kind of relationship. So she tried to evade. Not that it worked.

Logan's dark eyes sharpened and he leaned closer to her. "You don't have to lie about dating someone, Megan. I'd think Mom and Dad would be happy about that. If you got married, then they'd know you were at least taken care of."

Megan looked back at him, eyes blazing, heat rushing through her body from the intensity of her anger and frustration. "Who said anything about getting married? I dated a guy for a while this semester, but it wasn't ever anything close to serious. And why do I need to be taken care of? I've been doing a pretty good job taking care of myself for the last few years. I work, I pay my bills, I took out loans to go to school. Since I wouldn't bow to the family's wishes for my life, I haven't had any real help with money since I moved out the summer after I graduated. That's more than either of you could say at my age."

"I knew it! You were dating someone!" At Charlie's triumphant declaration, Megan turned her anger on him.

"Can it, Chuck. This is why I don't tell you things. This is why we don't talk anymore. Every word gets relayed back to Mom and Dad. If I wanted them to know I'd tell them myself."

"Hey, hey, let's all calm down." Logan, ever the peacemaker, put a hand on her shoulder but she brushed him off. "We care about you, Megan. We're on your side."

She snorted. "Please, Logan. I know you all think I'm some rebel who needs to be brought back into the fold, or at least some frail waif that needs to be taken care of."

"I don't think that at all. The only reason I've ever pushed for you to change your major is because I want you to be able to support yourself. Art isn't—"

"Realistic. Yeah, I know. I've heard it all before. But you haven't even seen my work since you graduated from high school when I was still in middle school. You've never bothered to come to any of my shows. You have no idea that I've actually started to sell my paintings. For good money. And that I'm taking marketing and business classes so I can learn how to compete and find an audience. You know nothing about any of that." Megan was spitting mad now, but kept her voice low so their parents wouldn't come in and see what was wrong. "You know nothing about my life, so just stay out of it. I can take care of myself just fine."

Logan opened his mouth to say something, but she held up her hand, palm out, and he stopped. "Just do me a favor, okay? When this stuff comes up at dinner, and we all know it will, just stay out of it." She let her gaze encompass Charlie as well. "Both of you. If you're not going to support me, fine. But at least don't help them tear me down."

Logan's brows drew down and he glowered at her for a moment, but whatever he was about to say was interrupted by their mother's voice from the kitchen. "Dinner's ready!"

The three of them filed into the dining room in silence and took their usual places—Charlie and Megan on the side by the wall, Logan at the foot, leaving the head of the table for their dad and the other side for their mom.

Her mom brought a basket of rolls into the dining room followed by her dad carrying a platter of sliced turkey. They both set their burdens in the places reserved for them on the table and were about to take their seats when the doorbell rang.

Her dad's head popped up. "Karen, did you invite someone and forget to tell us?"

Her mom shook her head. "No. Obviously you didn't either. Kids?" They all stared blankly at each other, Megan and her brothers shaking their heads.

"Well, I guess I'll go see who it is." Her dad made his way to the front door. They could hear low voices, but couldn't make out what was being said.

"Megan! Could you come out here, please?" Her dad's voice was laced with barely restrained irritation. What could possibly be going on now?

Megan stood, squeezed behind Charlie's chair, and went out to the foyer through the living room. "What is it, Dad?"

He stepped out of the way, revealing Chris standing in the open doorway, backlit by the sun lowering on the horizon, even though it wasn't even three in the afternoon. It was one of those rare clear and sunny days in November, but twilight came early this time of year. Megan stopped in her tracks, not sure what was going on.

Chris hunched his shoulders, his hands in his pockets, looking more uncomfortable than she'd ever seen him. He usually had an easy manner and got along with most people. Never awkward or uncomfortable. "Hey, Megan."

Her dad stood with his arms crossed and stared at her. She looked back and forth between him and

Chris before settling on Chris. "Hey, Chris. What are you doing here?"

"Uh, I needed to talk to you." He shifted on his feet, but held her gaze.

"You couldn't use a phone?" Her dad's arch tone cut through the tension stringing between them, and Chris's eyes cut sideways. He shrugged, but didn't say anything. Megan was kind of glad that he didn't bring up that she'd been ignoring his calls and texts, because that would've opened up another line of questioning that she didn't want to deal with right now.

"Richard, Megan, invite the boy in for dinner." Her mom's voice carried from the living room, where she was peering through the doorway to see what was going on.

Chris held up his hands, palms out. "Oh, I'm sorry. I didn't realize you were about to eat. I'll—I'll go." His eyes flicked to her dad and mom, but settled again on Megan.

Megan didn't say anything, just stood there, unsure how she was supposed to respond to this. Her mom didn't have any such qualm. "Nonsense. We have plenty of food. You're obviously a friend of Megan's and you're not home with your own family. Come in. Richard, grab the extra chair."

Megan turned and followed her mom back to the dining room, acutely aware of Chris trailing behind her.

"Charlie, get up. Your dad's getting another chair. Megan and her friend will sit over there and you can sit on this side by me."

Charlie stood from his seat and moved around the head of the table, his eyes flicking between Megan and Chris the whole time. Megan could feel the weight of Logan's gaze on her as well, but she kept her eyes on the chair she was going to sit in, and stared at her empty plate after she sat down.

Her dad came in a moment later with a folding chair for Charlie. They passed around the food in silence. Megan tried to avoid Chris's eye, but couldn't stop her fingers from brushing his as they passed bowls and serving dishes back and forth.

The first part of the meal passed in tense silence. At least it felt that way to Megan. Unasked questions about Chris and why he was there seemed to dominate the room. Her parents and brothers kept looking at them, watching their interactions or lack thereof. Add that to the underlying tension already present between her and her family, and this was the most uncomfortable Thanksgiving on record.

Finally, her mom broke the silence. She cleared her throat. "I'd like it if we all went around and said something we were thankful for. Richard, would you start?"

Dad nodded. "I'm thankful that business has been going well this year."

Mom pursed her lips in slight disappointment at such a generic statement, but let it go. "I'm thankful to have all of our kids home for Thanksgiving this year for the first time since Logan graduated from college."

"I'm thankful for all this delicious food." Charlie shoveled a huge bite of mashed potatoes into his mouth.

Their mom playfully smacked his arm. "Be serious."

"I am!" he protested. At least, that's what Megan thought he said. It was hard to tell with his mouth half full. She couldn't help smiling and heard Chris chuckle quietly beside her.

Logan cleared his throat and shot a quelling glance at his younger brother. "I'm thankful that my internship turned into me getting hired at my firm." Their dad nodded his approval, his pride in his oldest son's career and accomplishments evident from his demeanor.

Great, now it was Megan's turn. She finished chewing slowly, casting about for something to say. She didn't feel all that thankful for anything on that particular day, or even that week. "I'm thankful for good friends." There, that seemed general enough to not give anything away to her family about what was going on in her life, but specific enough to make her mom happy. Her parents had no idea she hadn't been living with Abby since August, much less that she'd been seeing Chris. And she had no desire for that to change.

All eyes turned to Chris, who shifted in his seat. "Um, I'm thankful for good friends too." He glanced at her out of the corner of his eye before he returned his attention to his plate, now only half full of food.

"No, no, no. That's cheating. You have to say something no one else has said."

Megan glared at her brother. "Shut up, Charlie. He's a guest. He doesn't even have to participate if he doesn't want to."

Charlie made a derisive noise. "Your boyfriend can come to his own defense. Come on. What else are you thankful for?"

Megan wished she could maim her brother with her eyes. She didn't want to kill him, just incapacitate him enough that he couldn't talk anymore today. Before she could say anything, Chris spoke up.

"I'm thankful for Megan. She's helping me pass several of my classes and I wouldn't have managed to without her."

Megan covered her face with her hands and let out a soft groan. That was not what she was hoping for.

"Really, Megan?" Her mom's voice was filled with interest.

Megan put her hands down. "I told you that I work in the tutoring center. I'm tutoring him." It was technically true, even if she didn't meet with him in the tutoring center.

Logan's eyes were full of speculation. "How interesting that one of your clients would decide to crash our Thanksgiving." He shifted his gaze to Chris. "What else is going on between you two? Why did you come here today?"

Megan's mouth fell open in shock. Her family was usually all about proper behavior and politeness. Apparently law school had burned that out of Logan. She turned to Chris. "Ignore him. You don't have to answer that. He thinks he gets to question everyone now because he's a lawyer. He just found out he passed the bar last week, so he's got a fat head." She glared at Logan and mouthed, "Shut up," at him behind her hand.

"No, Megan, he's got a point." Now it was Charlie's turn to jump in. "I think we all want to know why he's here."

Megan looked to her parents for help, but she should've known better than to do that. Her mom's face was impassive, a study in neutrality, looking to her husband for his reaction before she had an opinion of her own.

Her dad set down his napkin next to his plate and sat back in his chair. "You know, I think the boys are right. Why are you here, young man?"

"You don't have to answer that, Chris." Megan met his eyes, not sure if she wanted him to answer or not. She wanted to know why he'd come, but she didn't want to hash everything out in front of her whole family. They needed to talk for sure, but not here, not like this. Damn, but she wished she'd taken at least one of his calls now.

He held her gaze. "No, that's alright. I don't mind. I'm surprised it took this long for anyone to ask me." He turned his head, sweeping his gaze across the table before he looked back at Megan. "I've missed you and needed to see you again. Things went ..." he trailed off, his eyes glancing around the table again before continuing, "strangely on Saturday. And you didn't give me a chance to explain."

"So you crashed my house on Thanksgiving?" Megan was trying to keep her voice down, so she was practically hissing out her response. "I thought you were going home. Why aren't you there?"

He shrugged. "I did go home, but I couldn't stay there without seeing you and talking to you. You need to give me a chance to tell you what happened."

"I already know what happened. It doesn't matter. You shouldn't have come."

"Megan?" Megan turned to face her mom, realizing how intent everyone was on their conversation. "This sounds like a private matter. Would you prefer to go discuss it in your bedroom?"

"Karen!" Her dad looked scandalized that her mom would suggest she take a boy into her bedroom alone. Megan would've laughed under any other circumstances.

She shook her head. "No, Mom. We don't need to go in the other room. There's nothing more to talk about. Let's just finish eating, okay? Isn't there apple pie for later?"

Her mom's eyes examined her face for a moment before she nodded gracefully. "Yes, there's apple, pumpkin, and pecan. There's also whipped cream and ice cream to go with them. Of course, we'll wait a bit between dinner and dessert. I think the boys will want to finish watching whatever football game is on."

Megan's eyes flicked to her brothers, who were both scowling at Chris. Logan opened his mouth, but Megan glared daggers at him. He looked at their parents and whatever he saw there had him ducking his head and shoveling more food in his mouth. Charlie had kept eating regardless of his desire to scowl, but fortunately didn't feel the need to say anything.

Her dad wasn't put off by her attempt to change the subject. "Megan, what is the nature of your relationship with this boy?"

Oh, God. This was getting worse.

"We're dating." Chris's voice rang out confidently, causing Megan to cover her face with her hands.

"Oh, God. Just stop. Everybody stop." She muttered her words, but her dad heard her.

"Excuse me?" His rising voice gave away his anger. "We brought you up better than to take the Lord's name in vain. I can't stop you from talking however you like when you're not here, but in my home you will not do that. Do you understand me?" Megan nodded without looking up and her dad turned his attention back to Chris.

"Now, you say you're dating?"

Megan swore she could hear Chris swallowing. "Yes, sir." She wasn't sure where his manners had come from, but she didn't think they'd be enough to mollify her dad.

His tone deceptively calm, her dad continued to question Chris. "How did the two of you meet? Megan hasn't told us much about you, I'm afraid." Oh, God. If you didn't know better, you'd think he were being friendly and conversational. Megan knew better. Chris didn't. She felt him relax beside her.

"We met over the summer. Her friend Abby started dating Lance, my former roommate." Megan stifled another groan at that.

"Former roommate? What happened?" Her dad's voice still sounded normal, but Megan could see the shitstorm coming and she wasn't sure how to stop it. She had to try, though.

"Mom, dinner today is really good. Don't you think so, Dad?"

Her dad's dark eyes flicked to her. "Yes, of course. It's delicious as always. Thank you, dear." The last part was directed at her mom, before he turned back to Chris. "You were saying?"

Megan interrupted again. "Did I tell you I'm being featured in a show over Christmas?"

Her mom's eyebrows went up slightly, betraying her surprise. "No, honey. You didn't say anything. That's wonderful. Where?"

"There's an artist collective downtown that has shows every couple of weeks. I applied to be featured and just found out I was selected last week."

Her dad waved that away. "That's nice. But an artist collective isn't exactly the Guggenheim now is it?" He turned back to Chris whose mouth had fallen open at that comment. "Now, what happened with your former roommate?"

"He moved in with his girlfriend." Chris's response sounded automatic, his focus still on her dad's previous statement. "I'm sorry, did you just put down your daughter's art show because it's local?"

Lips compressed in disapproval, her dad waved that question away as well. "He moved in with his girlfriend?" His eyes flicked to Megan. "But he just said Abby is his friend's girlfriend. Isn't Abby your roommate? So does he live with you too?"

Megan groaned and covered her face again. This just kept getting worse.

"No, Megan took over Lance's place in our house. Back to her art show."

"What?" Her dad shot out of his chair, his face thunderous. He pointed a finger at Megan. "You mean to tell me you've been living with this boy? Since when?"

Chris opened his mouth and looked between Megan and her dad. Megan had never seen Chris look at such a loss before. He wasn't sure what to say, and Megan almost felt bad for him. Almost.

She sighed, straightened her shoulders, and held her head up. It was out now. The only thing for it was to brazen through. Maybe this was a good thing in some way. At least now she wouldn't have to hide her living situation from her parents anymore. Even if it was changing soon.

"I moved in at the end of August when Abby and Lance decided to move in together. I needed a place to live and Chris and Matt had a room they needed filled. It worked out for everyone."

Megan heard her mom let out a little gasp, but kept her eyes trained on her father. His face was getting redder by the second.

"You live with two boys?"

"I grew up in a house with two boys. I fail to see the problem."

"They're your brothers! It's completely different!" Her dad was in a towering rage now. He slammed his palm on the table. "You will move home this instant! I'll send your brothers to collect your things. If this is what that college does to you, then you will not be going back!"

Megan stood up and leaned over the table. She stared at him, not breaking his gaze, her muscles clenched so hard she was almost shaking. "No." She said it quietly, her voice hard and full of determination.

Her dad jerked back in shock. "Excuse me? You do not tell me no!"

"I just did. I pay all my bills. I'm an adult. You can't order me to move back home and expect me to obey anymore. Maybe you should've thought of that before refusing to help me out financially when I didn't do what you wanted the first time."

Chris's hand on her back drew her attention to the fact that he was on his feet next to her. He leaned in closer to her ear. "Come on, Megan. You don't need this shit. Let's go."

She tore her eyes away from her dad for a moment and looked at Chris. His hazel eyes were sincere and apologetic, his mouth in a tight line betraying his anger on her behalf. At least this man supported her, thought she could make it as an artist, and cared about her for herself instead of for how her actions might reflect on her family. That was what was really behind her dad's blustering. If anyone at her parents' church found out she was living with a man she wasn't related to or married to, it wouldn't look good for her family. But she'd long ago stopped caring enough about what other people thought to let it dictate her life. Too bad her parents couldn't get on the same page.

"Young man, you can leave if you like, but Megan's staying. I'd say it was nice to meet you, but I don't like lying." Megan's dad sounded even more pompous than usual. Chris ignored him.

Megan's eyes bounced between her dad and Chris. She still didn't want to be alone with Chris, but she couldn't stand being here any more. It was abundantly clear that her parents would never approve of her. She had to get out of here. Decision made, she nodded once, and took the hand he held out.

Her mom gasped, a hand flying to her mouth. Her dad's face contorted in further expressions of fury. Who knew he could manage that? "Megan, if you walk out with him, you're not welcome here anymore."

"Richard!" Her mom's face was horror stricken and her voice little more than a whisper. The set of her dad's face made it clear he wouldn't give an inch.

Megan looked from him to her mom. "Thanks for dinner, Mom. You're welcome to call if you ever want to check in and see how I'm doing. Bye."

Chris's fingers squeezed hers, offering his strength through their connection. Her eyes fixed ahead, she led the way out of the dining room, grabbing her jacket and backpack on her way to the front door. Her trepidation at being alone with Chris was more than outweighed by the relief of leaving her parents' house.

Chapter Twenty-One

"Where are we going?"

Chris glanced at Megan in the passenger seat. Even though she'd spoken, she faced forward, her eyes glued to the scenery out the windshield, her arms crossed tightly over her torso.

"I'm not sure. I don't really know my way around here. And it's Thanksgiving. Is there anything open?"

Megan shook her head. "I don't know."

Chris was silent for a moment, trying to figure out how this would work. He had a cauldron of emotion bubbling in his chest, and he wasn't sure how to deal with everything. He was still furious with the way Megan's parents had treated her. Demanding she move back home and acting like her art was a joke. That would be like his parents making fun of him for going to the Regional Combines and telling him his hopes of going pro were stupid and not to be taken seriously. He couldn't imagine how awful that would be. His parents were happy for him to take the chance. And if he didn't make it, they'd still have his back.

He was glad that she'd come with him. When she'd stared at him after he'd suggested they leave he was worried that she wouldn't come with him, that maybe she'd just cave in to her parents, and he'd be left looking like an idiot by meekly sitting back down, or a jerk by storming out alone.

Adrenaline still coursed through his blood stream after the confrontation they'd just left, adding to the nerves already brewing about finally getting to talk to Megan. It made him want to take the curving roads down the hill at the edge of town much faster than he should, especially with the temperature dropping and ice in the forecast. He took a deep breath and tried to will himself to calm down.

"I'd like to go somewhere we can talk. After that I'll take you back to get your car."

He watched Megan out of the corner of his eye, splitting his attention between her and the road. She pursed her lips before nodding and blowing out a breath. "Fine. We can talk. I doubt anywhere's open, so let's just go downtown and park by the lake."

"Okay. Just tell me where to go."

One side of her mouth turned up, but that was the only expression, and it was gone as soon as it appeared. She gave him directions in a soft monotone until they were driving along a treed one-lane road, the local community college on the left and the mouth of the river flowing away from the lake stretching out to the right. They drove until they were in front of the lake itself, tall pines towering above them on both sides of the road.

"Pull over here." She gestured toward the left side of the road.

"On the left?"

Megan nodded. "The right side is the Centennial Trail. It's for pedestrians and cyclists. Parking's on the left on the dike road." She was silent for a moment, looking around. "It looks so thin. I can't believe they took out so many trees."

"What?" He couldn't make sense of her cryptic comments. They were there to talk about what happened on Saturday and why she'd run away and not returned his calls, and she wanted to talk about trees?

She gestured around. "There used to be a lot more trees. They took out like seventy percent of them in the summer and fall. They were only supposed to thin thirty percent. Apparently they got carried away." The wistfulness in her tone turned to acidic sarcasm on the last sentence.

Chris made a noncommittal hum. He really wasn't sure what the point of this conversation was, but he let her talk. At least she wasn't freezing him out with silence. Finally she turned and looked at him, her expression solemn, guarded. Not the usual openness with the hint of a smile playing around her lips that he was used to.

Her eyes examined his face. "Why did you come today?"

"You wouldn't take my calls. I needed to talk to you."

She cocked her head to one side. "Most people would take my lack of response as a sign that I don't want to talk to them."

"That's not fair, Megan. I deserve a chance to explain at least. If you're going to break up with me, have the balls to do it in person. Don't just leave and freeze me out." His hands still rested on the steering wheel, and he squeezed it hard, transferring his frustration and nerves to the inanimate object instead of taking it out on Megan. At least he managed to keep his voice controlled.

She studied him for another moment before nodding once. "You're right. I'm sorry." She looked away and stared at the trees across the water. "You don't need to explain, though. Lance told me what happened."

"He did?" His voice came out strangled and he cleared his throat. "What did he tell you?"

"That you didn't do anything wrong. That that chick climbed onto your lap while you were almost asleep and started kissing you. That you dumped her off your lap and told her off in front of everyone then came looking for me."

That about summed it up. He let out a breath, grateful that Lance had at least been there to tell his side of things. "When did he tell you that?"

He saw her close her eyes, but she still wouldn't face him. "Sunday."

"So you've known the truth since Sunday, but you've still refused to talk to me." He paused, waiting for a reaction, a little surprised himself that he was still managing to keep his voice low and even instead of yelling, or getting out of the car and punching a tree or throwing rocks into the water. Those things still weren't out of the question, but he really wanted to finish this conversation before he gave into that urge. He'd been managing to keep his temper in check by spending lots of time in the weight room the last few days. Sadly all the university buildings were closed up the rest of the week, including the weight room. He wouldn't be able to go work off his frustration once he was done here. Not until Monday. Shit.

Megan gave the barest nod in answer to his question, her eyes still closed, like she was bracing herself for his reaction.

He squeezed the steering wheel harder. "Care to tell me why?"

She opened her eyes to blink rapidly a few times and looked up at the roof of the car. "I'm not upset about Saturday anymore. I know that wasn't your fault and you didn't do anything wrong. Regardless, we can't continue seeing each other. I'm sorry."

"What?" The even control was gone. He was in shock, and the word flew out at almost full volume before he could stop it. "What the fuck does that mean?"

Megan closed her eyes again, still refusing to look at him. Her voice stayed soft and steady. "I'm sorry. But it's for the best." She uncrossed her arms and reached for the door handle. "The Resort's just on the other side of the park around that curve. I'll walk there and get one of my brothers to come get me. I'll be in touch about moving my things. I'll pay for December's rent so you guys have enough time to find a new roommate."

She had opened the door as she finished her sentence, and already had one foot outside, intending to walk somewhere in the twilight. Chris grabbed her other arm and stopped her before she could get out all the way. "What the fuck are you talking about?"

"Let me go, Chris." Her eyes were glued to his fingers wrapped around her arm. The fabric of her coat kept him from feeling her warmth.

The fact that she was so still and calm was almost more infuriating than what she was saying. He'd seen lots of sides to Megan. She almost always let everyone know exactly what she thought. She didn't hold back and didn't pull punches. This still calmness hid something much more turbulent, he was sure of it. Something she didn't want him to see.

"No. Look me in the eyes and say that again. And don't forget to explain why." He managed not to yell, but his voice sounded harsh and commanding.

She raised her eyes to his, and they glistened with suppressed tears in the waning light. "I can't see you anymore. I'm sorry." Her eyelids dropped and a tear slid down her left cheek. Before he could react she'd wrenched her arm out of his slackened grip and gotten out of the car. The slam of the door brought him back to himself. He yanked the keys out of the ignition and got out, going after her.

He only had to jog a few steps before he caught up to her, the pine needles on the asphalt crunching under his feet. He grabbed her by the shoulders and whirled her around. His chest squeezed when he saw the tears streaming down her face and breathing became more difficult. She uncrossed her arms, scrubbing at her red eyes and nose with her hands, wiping away the tears, then lifted her chin. It was the same defiant tilt to her head she'd used when she was going at it with her dad before they'd left.

Chris gripped her shoulders, not letting her go so she couldn't walk away from him again. "No. That's not good enough. You can't freeze me out for almost a week and then give me the brush off when we finally talk. I deserve better than that from you." He managed to restrain himself a little so he didn't shake her to make a point, but his fingers dug into the thick fabric of her coat. "And you can't go back to your family. They'll make you leave school and give up your art. You can't do that."

The defiant look softened a little and her brows crinkled together. She sniffed, reaching up and rubbing her nose again. "Why do you care so much?" Her curls bounced as she shook her head, not giving him a chance to answer her question. She took a step back and broke his grip. "I can't do this anymore, Chris. I just—" She looked away over the water for a moment, the sun little more than an orange glow over the hills ringing the lake, searching for words. "This semester's been fun, but we both know it's not going anywhere. I'm going to be really busy next semester with all my upper level classes." She raised her face, closing her eyes. "And I need to find a roommate and a new place to live." When she looked back at him, her eyes were clear again, the iron control that Chris hadn't known she possessed back in place. "See?" A small smile curved her lips, but didn't lighten the sadness of her face. "I've got a lot to do, so I'll just head over there." She gestured behind her to where the road curved, leading to the resort she'd mentioned. "The walk will help me sort things out and my brothers will either bring me my car, or pick me up and take me back to it." She tried to smile again, but it didn't seem to be working very well. "Thanks for everything. I guess I'll see you around."

Chris waited through this rambling monologue, grinding his teeth in frustration. When she turned to walk away again, he caught her arm once more. "Dammit, Megan. Stop walking away from me. I'm not done talking to you."

She drew in a ragged breath. "Why? Just let me go, Chris. Let me walk away. I can't do this anymore. This is killing me. Just let me go."

He pulled her closer, reeling her in by his grip on her arm, and she went, unresisting. He wrapped his arms around her and looked down into her face. "Why do you keep pushing me away? Tell me what's really going on. And don't sell me that line about school being busy. We both know that's a bullshit excuse. You said you're not mad at me about Saturday. That you know I didn't do anything. If that's not what this is about, then what is it?"

She didn't say anything. She just buried her face against the fabric of his sweatshirt. Her whole body shuddered against him again and again. Warm wetness seeped through his clothes and made its way to his chest.

"Megan? You're freaking me out here. Talk to me. What's going on?"

She drew another shuddering breath before lifting her face and pushing back. He relaxed his hold on her so she could put some space between them, but didn't let go entirely. She kept her face down, running her hands over her face, wiping her cheeks. Her eyes flicked up to his face, but focused on the wet spot on his sweatshirt from her tears. "Look, I know this was just supposed to be casual. I know you don't do relationships and this worked out as long as it did because we live together and it's super convenient. Plus, you were gone a lot during the season, so it was easier to not get bored. But you'll be home all the time now, and you're sure to get bored sooner or later, and I really won't be able to handle it if you start hooking up with other chicks while we're still roommates. So, let's just end this now, like adults."

Chris's hands tightened around her elbows, where he still held on to her. "You think I'm going to get bored?" He couldn't keep the incredulity out of his voice. "That's why you're breaking up with me? You're leaving me first so I don't leave you?"

"No, that's not—" She cut herself off, putting her hands on his chest and pushing a little. "I just— This just isn't working for me anymore, okay? I can't do this."

"What can't you do? What's not working? There's something you're not telling me. Something you've been keeping from me since the Halloween party. What happened there? I don't want this to end. If something's wrong, tell me, and we can fix it. Don't just walk away."

She wrapped her arms around herself and tucked her chin down, withdrawing. "I can't be your convenient fuck buddy anymore. I want more than that. Just let me go."

He flinched and dropped his hands, giving in to her request to let her go at last. "A convenient fuck buddy? Is that what you think you are? Is that what you think I am?" His voice grew louder with each question. The wind off the lake picked up, slicing through his sweatshirt, freezing the wet spot on his chest.

Megan put out a hand, almost like she was reaching for him, but she dropped it. "Don't you?" Her tone sounded almost pleading. "If that's not what I am to you, then what am I?"

He put his hands in his pockets, trying to adopt a casual stance and expression, but the harshness of his voice ruined the effect. "Well, I sort of thought you were my girlfriend."

Megan looked stunned. Her mouth fell open and she froze. "Really?"

The tortured hope in that one whispered word almost broke Chris's heart. He reached for her, and she didn't back away or try to escape. "What did you think was going on? You said you wanted to be exclusive way back in September. That usually means girlfriend, doesn't it? Did I miss something?" Chris pulled her in closer, holding her against him again, driving out the cold with her warmth.

She had her hands over her mouth and shook her head. "We never defined anything. I didn't want to assume. And then at the Halloween party, someone was saying—" She shook her head again. "Never mind. It doesn't matter."

He squeezed her. "Yes it does. What happened? What did someone say?"

"Someone told me that you were only with me because I was a convenient fuck. Having me in the house saved you from having to go out and find someone to hook up with. That you'd get tired of me sooner than later, especially once the season ended."

Chris's fingers tightened in the fabric of Megan's coat, his jaw clenching again. "Who said that?"

She shook her head. "I don't know. Some girl. It was when I went looking for Matt, Lance, and Abby at the party. I'd checked all the back rooms and was headed back to the living room when I saw the girl in the slutty devil costume hitting on you. A redhead dressed as a Playboy bunny came up next to me and started talking."

Chris closed his eyes and let out a breath. "That's why you started doing shots in the kitchen?"

She nodded, not meeting his eyes again. "It made sense. What she said made terrible sense, and I couldn't get the idea out of my head."

God, what had she been thinking? Believing some jealous bitch at a party instead of the evidence in front of her? He rushed home to her every night, texted her and called her as much as possible when he was out of town. Hell, he even did homework with her. If that didn't seem like a commitment, he didn't know what did. "You know I turned the slutty devil down, don't you?" He waited for her nod before he continued. "Why didn't you talk to me about it? You of all people should know better than to listen to gossip at a party."

Her eyes came up then, wariness settling on her face. "What do you mean by that? What have people been saying about me?" She started to push away again, but Chris tightened his arms, not letting her get away.

"That Isaac motherfucker has been running his mouth all semester. You know the kinds of things he was saying over the summer. He hadn't been given a reason to stop yet. He has now."

"What does that mean?" She'd stopped trying to get away, but the wariness hadn't left her face.

"I overheard him talking to his friends earlier this week. I convinced him that continuing to talk about you wasn't in his best interests."

"Did you beat the shit out of him?" Her gaze was direct and unflinching. He couldn't bring himself to dodge the question.

He shrugged one shoulder. "Not quite. He could still walk when I was done, but he got the point."

Chris felt Megan deflating in his arms. She rested her forehead on his chest for a minute, and he relished the feeling of her in his arms again. Letting him hold her. He'd missed holding her this last week. So much.

She lifted her head. "You didn't need to do that."

"Yes, I did." He said it definitively, wanting to end any argument about this before it could start. "I'm never going to stand quietly by while some asshole talks shit about my girlfriend. Especially when I know what he's saying is a goddamn lie." Megan's eyes grew wide, but he didn't let her say anything. He'd let her talk enough already. And he was tired of listening to this bullshit about how she thought she was just a convenient fuck buddy that didn't mean anything to him. If his actions hadn't been enough to show how he felt, then he'd damn well better lay it out for her.

"How do you not know that you're more to me than just a fuck buddy? I spend every free moment with you. Which, admittedly isn't a lot during football season between practice and workouts and class. But fuck buddies don't talk every night they're apart. They don't do homework together."

"But we're also roommates, so doing homework together isn't that ridiculous."

Chris gave Megan a stern look for interrupting, especially to say that. "Do you think I'd do homework with you if you were just my roommate? Did I ever do that before we got together?" She shook her head and opened her mouth, but he kissed her, wanting to stop her from saying something stupid again. She stiffened at first, but softened under his mouth, opening for him, letting him deepen the kiss. She was more passive than normal, lacking the participation and enthusiasm that he'd grown used to, but at least she didn't pull away or slap him. The icy lump in his stomach that had taken up residence on Saturday night began to thaw and the tightness in his chest relaxed, warmth spreading through him.

He finally broke the kiss and rested his forehead against hers. "Do you really not know how I feel about you?"

Her dark brown eyes stared into his, not breaking his gaze as she shook her head. "Tell me."

"I've been going crazy since you left the party Saturday. Abby delayed me so I couldn't get out of there to talk to you and Lance wouldn't let me see you that night at all. You wouldn't return my calls or texts and all I've been able to think about is getting to you so I could explain what happened and beg you to forgive me. I even waited outside the tutoring center on Monday hoping I could catch you there. I went home yesterday like I'd planned, but the whole way to Port Orchard I just kept thinking about how wrong it was that I'd left without talking to you, without seeing you, without saying goodbye. I wanted to take you home with me to meet my family. My sister and her husband are there, and I know she'd get a kick out of you. She already thinks it's hilarious that some girl has got me going to classes and doing homework and set up to graduate in May."

"You want me to meet your family?" Her eyes glittered with moisture again, and he sucked in a breath, worried about why she was starting to cry again, but decided to plow on.

"Of course. I just wasn't sure if you'd want to come. You never talk about your family. I didn't even know you were from here. I just assumed you were going home for Thanksgiving, so I didn't want to put you on the spot by inviting you to come home with me. I didn't think about it until I was on my way and everything just felt so wrong without you there. I'm tired of leaving you behind while I go out of town. I miss you when I'm gone. I don't sleep as well without you in my arms."

Chris took a deep breath, prepared to go on, but stopped when he saw tears making their way down her cheeks. "What's wrong?"

She shook her head and let out a choked laugh. "I don't sleep well without you, either. Why didn't you tell me any of this before? I thought— God, I already told you what I thought. I've been falling for you for weeks and I assumed you didn't feel the same way. I couldn't continue seeing you, knowing that you didn't care about me as much as I care about you. I've stopped myself from telling you I love you more times than I can count."

The air grew solid and time stood still. Chris couldn't breathe. Megan loved him. She just said she loved him. Is that what this was called? This feeling that you could never get enough of another person? Like you were missing a piece of yourself when you were apart?

The mysterious thickening of the air vanished and he sucked in a breath. "I love you." He was breathing hard now, like he'd been playing an entire football game by himself. "Oh, God, Megan. You have no idea how much I love you."

This time she kissed him, her mouth crashing into his. He crushed her to his chest and her arms went around his neck. They stayed locked together until a car drove up and honked at them for standing in the middle of the road. They broke apart, sheepish smiles on their faces, and moved back toward Chris's car, offering apologetic waves to the driver.

Chris held open Megan's door and closed it behind her after she climbed in.

"Take me home," she said when he got into the driver's seat.

"What about your car?"

"I'll ask my brothers to bring it to me or we can go get it tomorrow. I don't care. I just don't want to be apart right now." She shot him a smile, but her face was serious.

He reached over and held her hand, maneuvering the car with his left. "That's fine with me." He was breathing easier than he had in almost a week. He'd drive Megan around himself and leave her car at her parents' house forever if it meant they were together.

Megan stumbled after Chris as he practically dragged her through the door. He whirled around once he was inside, pulled her in, and slammed the door behind her. With a flick of his fingers he locked the door and pushed her against it.

"God, I've missed you." His mouth crashed onto hers, firm and demanding, all the softness and exploration from earlier when they were by the lake gone.

Megan's hands went to his shoulders, first clutching him by the fabric of his sweatshirt, then pushing him back. "Where's Matt?"

With his face only inches from hers, she could watch the minute details of Chris's expressions. Confusion passed over his face before the haze of lust lifted from his eyes for a moment after he processed her question. "Still in Westport, I'm pretty sure. Why?"

"I thought you guys were driving over there together, so if you're here I was just wondering if he came home too."

Chris shook his head. "We drove separately. I haven't been very good company this week. Matt didn't want to be stuck in a car with me for six or seven hours. Can we stop talking about Matt now?"

A smile stretched her lips wide and she nodded. Chris's mouth was on hers again, his tongue sweeping into her mouth, tangling with hers. Megan sucked on it, which made Chris groan. His hands slid under her jacket and around her back, then down below her ass to lift her. She wrapped her legs around his waist and hung on while he pinned her to the door and rocked his hips against hers. She could feel his cock, hard and ready, through the fabric of their jeans.

She turned her head, breaking their kiss. Unfazed, he kissed down along her jawline to her ear, sucked the lobe into his mouth, and scraped his teeth over the sensitive skin. She gasped. "Chris. I need you. Now."

He lifted his head, a cocky grin on his lips, and kissed her hard once more before he pulled her away from the door and carried her into their room. Their room. She'd stopped herself from calling it that before, even in her own head. It had always been her room, and the other bedroom that he never slept in was Chris's room. Even though most of his clothes had migrated into her room a long time ago, she hadn't let herself think of him as sharing her room because that implied more of a commitment than she thought they had.

Chris tossed her onto the bed. Their bed. Megan couldn't wipe the smile off her face.

Chris yanked his sweatshirt and t-shirt off together, standing before her in just his jeans, an answering smile on his face. "What are you smiling about?"

Megan shook her head. She felt stupid trying to explain, so she didn't. "Nothing. Everything. I'm just happy to be here again with you."

He crawled over her, the look in his eyes that of a predator stalking his prey. Megan shivered in anticipation despite the fact that she still wore her cashmere sweater and a wool coat. Chris laid himself on top of her and fitted himself between her thighs. He pressed her down into the mattress, bracing himself on his arms so he didn't crush her. He kissed her hard then pulled back to look down into her face. His hazel eyes looked like a ring of gold surrounding the darkness of his dilated pupils. "I'm happy you're here again, too. I'd be even happier if you weren't wearing so many clothes."

Her mouth curved into a wicked grin to match his own. "It's hard to get undressed with you on top of me."

He hummed in agreement before he kissed her again, sat back on his knees, and pulled her up with him. "Get undressed. Now. I'm tired of waiting."

Megan opened her mouth to argue, but closed it again. They wanted the same thing, arguing with him wouldn't help her either. She pulled off her jacket and tossed it onto the floor. "Fine. You need to finish stripping too."

He grinned and stood up, undoing his belt, his eyes never leaving hers. She was topless before he'd gotten further than unzipping, and his eyes dropped to her naked chest. He leaned one knee on the bed again and reached for her, his hands running over her torso to cup her breasts. Her nipples hardened against his palms and he tweaked them with his fingers before lowering his head to suck one into his mouth. She hissed when he scraped his teeth over it, hard enough to sting a little, but immediately made better with firm pressure from his tongue. She clutched his head, her fingers tightening in his hair, arching into him. He sucked on her nipple, rubbing his tongue over it, and pulled back until he released it with a pop before switching to the other side.

After spending a few minutes there, he pulled back and looked down at her body, groaning. "You still have pants on."

"So do you."

He nodded absently, stood back up, and watched her fingers fall to the button of her pants. He pushed his own jeans and boxers down, his eyes never straying from her body. She pushed everything down, shimmying a little and taking her time, giving him a little show since he was watching so intently. With a whoosh the room spun and she found herself on her back, Chris yanking her pants and panties the rest of the way off her legs and tossing them over his shoulder without looking. They hit the top of the dresser and knocked a few things over with a clatter and a thunk as something fell to the floor.

His grin was a little sheepish, but soon turned wicked again as he pounced on her. She spread her legs while he situated himself between them again, in the same place he'd been minutes before when they'd both been clothed. She sighed. It was so much better when they were naked. His cock rubbed against her, the head bumping into her clit every time he moved.

He reached for the nightstand, pulled out a condom, and sat up again to roll it on. His hand went between her legs, sliding a finger inside her, spreading her wetness around, rubbing it into her clit, adding another finger. Tingles shot up her spine from the pressure of his fingers inside her and the way his thumb circled around her clit. She arched, moaning, enjoying the way he watched her reactions to him. Her hands trailed to her breasts and she tugged at her nipples. If possible, his eyes darkened further. He licked his lips, leaning forward and replacing one of her hands with his mouth. He pulled his fingers out and positioned his cock at her entrance. With one thrust, she was fully impaled.

She arched, welcoming his invasion. God, she'd missed this. She hadn't gone so many days in a row without him since they'd gotten together.

He threaded his fingers through hers, holding her hands above her head, his eyes never leaving hers. She wanted to close her eyes or turn away, the raw intimacy of their eye contact while he moved inside her so slowly and exquisitely almost too much, but the force of his gaze compelled her to stay. Each thrust made her gasp, almost crying out. She wrapped her legs around him to trap him with her body as much as he trapped her.

He brought his knees under him and released her hands. He wrapped his arms underneath her, levering her up and onto his lap, the new position causing him to sink in even further. She wrapped her arms around his neck and started to unwind her legs from around his back so she could plant her feet to get some leverage, but one of his hands smoothed down her leg, indicating that he wanted her legs around him still, so she left them there, rocking against him. He guided her movements, his hands under her ass, her arms on his shoulders helping her, but every thrust was slow and torturous. Finally when she wasn't sure how much longer she could take this slow pace, he leaned her back in his arms and picked up the tempo. One hand came around, cupping her face, his thumb placed just over her lips. She sucked it into her mouth, her tongue swirling around it and Chris sucked in a breath.

His thumb came out from between her lips wet and shiny. He ran his hand down her body, between her breasts, over her belly, until his palm rested on her mound. His thumb dipped between them, circling over her clit, his touch light, the pace slow. As his thrusts grew faster, the pressure from his thumb grew firmer, circling faster and faster until he pressed it against her clit on one hard thrust and she shattered, her head thrown back, eyes closed, her back arched over his arm, her hands still clutching at his shoulders and her legs tight around his waist.

After her orgasm passed, her limbs were limp and she had trouble holding onto Chris. He lay her back on the bed, taking her mouth in a searing kiss while he pounded into her, her legs still wrapped around him, until he followed her into that shuddering oblivion.

He collapsed half on top of her, his arms gathering her to his chest, their legs tangled together. They stayed that way until he started to grow soft, and with a groan, Chris got up, his fingers wrapped around the base of the condom.

When he crawled back into the bed with her, he gathered her against his chest again, and dropped a kiss on her mouth. "I hope you got plenty to eat because I don't plan on letting you out of bed until morning."

She smiled up at him. Warmth spread through her chest and a sense of rightness settled over her. "I can get on board with that plan." She kissed him back.

They ended up foraging in the kitchen after a few hours, reduced to cleaning out the back of the pantry and getting creative, promising each other they'd go to the grocery store the next day to buy the pies they'd missed that afternoon and stock up on real groceries. It was the best Thanksgiving Megan could remember.

Epilogue

Megan made her way down the steps of the Corbin Coliseum along with the rest of the graduation attendees. Mike, Chris's dad, led the way, his broad shoulders cutting a path through the crowd, making it easy for her to follow. They were on their way to the reception that was set up in the student center. Chris and his mom Sharon, who had been his escort in the ceremony to put his academic hood on him, were meeting them there rather than trying to find each other in the crowded coliseum.

Once outside, Mike turned toward Megan and let her catch up to walk beside him. He smiled down at her. "Thanks again for helping Chris get on track. I don't think he would've graduated without your help."

Megan waved away the compliment. "You keep thanking me. Chris was the one who decided to get serious and do it. He put in the work. I just helped him get organized."

"Still. Sharon and I appreciate what you've done for him." His eyes, the same hazel as Chris's, beamed down at her, matching the warm smile on his face. He draped an arm across her shoulders and squeezed her close for a second before he released her. Megan managed not to stiffen, getting more used to the casual displays of affection from Chris's parents that she'd never had from hers, especially not her own father. They were free with hugs, kisses on the cheek, and other gestures with Chris, and by extension Megan. As a couple, Mike and Sharon were often touching when they were together. Nothing gross, but they held hands and sat snuggled together on the couch. It was easy to see where Chris got his penchant for displays of affection with her.

Once inside the student center, they moved more slowly, both of them scanning the crowd until they found Chris and Sharon. Sharon hugged Megan when they approached, squeezing her tightly before releasing her and stepping next to Mike, who slid his arm around Sharon and pressed a kiss to her upturned mouth. Megan smiled when Chris did almost the same thing to her, though he had to bend over further.

Megan felt like a shrimp with Chris's family. She was average height, but Chris and his dad were both over six feet tall, and Sharon was at least five eight or five nine flat-footed, and she wore heels when she dressed up.

Megan reached up and touched the gold colored fabric around Chris's neck, signifying that he now held a Bachelor of Science degree in Exercise Science. She smiled up at him. "Congratulations."

"Thanks." He smiled back down at her. "Next May it'll be your turn. I'll be your escort and hood you."

Her breath caught for a moment, and she dropped her eyes back to the hood at his throat. "You might not be able to, though. You might be busy with the team."

Chris had done well at the Regional Combines in Phoenix and gotten an invite to the Super Regional. He'd been drafted the week before in the sixth round by the Washington Mountain Lions. He was ecstatic and they'd celebrated with a party with everyone that mattered that weekend. They'd decided to have their own private celebration and were leaving Monday for a week away together at a cabin in the woods now that he'd graduated. It was a little one bedroom luxury cabin with all the amenities, including a hot tub. Its isolation made it perfect. No roommates or other distractions, just time to spend together. Since they would be doing the long distance thing starting in July when Chris left for training camp, they wanted to capitalize on any and all time together that they could.

He tilted her chin up so she looked him in the eye again. "It'll be the off-season. I'll be back as soon as my team's done for the season. Even if we go all the way to the Super Bowl, I'll be home by Valentine's Day. You're not getting rid of me that easily."

"Megan, you know you can come stay with us when he has home games so you can go see him," put in Mike, drawing her attention.

Sharon nodded enthusiastically. "Of course. We won't take no for an answer."

Megan smiled. "Okay."

They made their way to the line for finger foods and cookies, chatting about Chris getting drafted. It was still such a new thing that it seemed surreal.

Megan had just filled her plate and was turning away from the table when Mike stepped next to her. "So, Chris tells me you had a solo art show at a local gallery recently."

Megan nodded, holding her hand in front of her mouth while she finished chewing and swallowing. "Yes. It went really well, actually. My advisor set it up with a friend of hers that owns a small gallery downtown. I sold about half of my paintings, and have a couple commissions for more."

She'd managed to follow through with the idea she'd had at the beginning of the year when she saw all the shirtless football players at the party. The studies in the lines of the body and contrasting skin tones had done very well. Chris and Matt and some of their friends had helped, posing for her along with some of the figure models she knew from her classes. She'd felt like an anatomy illustrator while she worked, but the end result was stunning according to all her professors.

Mike's eyes widened in admiration. "Wow. That's great." He leaned closer, his voice lowering. "Chris told us about the falling out with your parents. I hope you know that we'll be there for you the way families should." He straightened up. "Let us know when you have another show. Sharon and I would love to come. Especially next fall when Chris won't be able to attend as easily."

Megan smiled at him, blinking rapidly to hold back her tears. She'd never known how it felt to have parents who supported her choices. How nice it must have been for Chris to grow up with that. They were happy that he'd graduated at all and didn't care that his GPA was average or that he didn't get any honors. Her parents were disappointed with just about every choice she'd made since high school. When he'd told his parents about pursuing his dream of playing for the NFL, they'd offered to pay for his airfare to get to the Regional Combines. His dad had even flown down to support him at the Super Regional, not wanting him to go through the entire process alone.

Sharon joined them while Chris chatted with some of his former teammates that were also graduating. "What are we talking about?"

"Megan's art shows."

Sharon's face brightened, her blue eyes lighting up. "Oh, yes. I saw your paintings at the house. They're wonderful. Chris said your show went really well. Do you have another one lined up yet?"

Megan shook her head, her mouth full again.

"Well, tell us when you do. And when you come visit, I'll see if I can introduce you to my client who owns an art gallery in Bremerton. She's always on the lookout for new talent." Sharon worked as a CPA and she had clients all over the Kitsap Peninsula, many of whom she also counted as friends.

Megan's heart fluttered. Who would've guessed that her boyfriend's parents would help her art career. "Thank you. That would be amazing. I don't know when we'll be over that way next, but I'll make a special effort to come if you set that up."

Sharon waved a hand. "Of course. Anything we can do to help. I'll send Janice an email later and see when she has openings she needs to fill."

Megan was blown away. Never had anyone just randomly offered her support and connections like this. Her art professors helped and supported her, but that was expected. Since her own parents didn't support her art pursuits, she didn't expect anyone else's parents to do so, much less offer to connect her with someone who could help advance her career.

Although, Megan's mom had come to her show. Alone. They'd spoken briefly and neither of them had mentioned Megan's dad. It was clear from her mom's attitude that he still wasn't acknowledging her. She hadn't stayed long, but it was something, and Megan recognized it for the olive branch it was. Her mom had started calling a few times a month to check in since Thanksgiving. Their conversations were short and only happened when Megan's dad wasn't home, but it was more contact than they'd had for almost a year prior to that. Megan appreciated the strength it took for her mom to go against her dad's wishes. She couldn't think of a time when that had ever happened before.

Her relationship with her brothers had stayed about the same—occasional phone calls on birthdays and major holidays. The big difference was that now they'd stopped trying to convince her to listen to their parents and at least refrained from commenting when she'd tell them about her art shows. Logan had seemed impressed with her successes the last time they'd talked.

They stayed at the reception for another hour or so before they headed back to the house they still shared with Matt so Chris could change out of his graduation regalia before they all went out for dinner to celebrate. Chris's parents went to their hotel to freshen up a little.

Chris tossed his cap and gown on the couch before pulling Megan in for a kiss. "I can't believe this is going to be my last summer in this house," he said when he broke away. "We'll have to look for a place together before I go to training camp. That way Matt can get his own place, too."

Megan gave him a coy smile. "What if Matt and I are planning on staying roommates."

Chris's hands on her sides tightened possessively, and he narrowed his eyes at her. "Huh-uh. Nope. You're my little roomie, and I can't wait until we don't have to share a place with anyone else. And with my signing bonus and the salary for next season we can get a nice place for us."

The smile slid off of Megan's face. She smoothed the placket of the black button-down shirt he'd worn under his regalia. "I still feel weird letting you pay for it all yourself."

He sighed. "We already went over this. You need to save your money for school, especially since you won't let me help with that. I want to rent a place for us to stay together. I'd be renting a place here to be able to be with you anyway. This way you won't have to find another roommate. It's the most sensible thing to do, and it makes me happy."

His grin was infectious, bringing a smile to her face, but only for a moment before she grew serious once more. "It's going to be hard having you gone for so long."

He wrapped his arms around her waist, pulling her more tightly against him. "I know. But it's only for like six months, and we'll see each other as often as we can. I'll come back once the season's over, and we'll be together here until you're done with school. Then we'll get a place in Seattle. You can build more contacts and paint while I play football."

She nodded. They'd been talking about this ever since he got drafted. It was a good plan. She liked their plan. She was just nervous because everything was changing so much. This was her first serious relationship and the stress of being long distance, even if only for a definite period of time, would be a big strain. Chris believed they could do it, and things had been great between them so far, so there was no reason to doubt.

Megan sighed and leaned her head against him. Things were changing, but it was for the better. Matt had a great new job and a steady girlfriend (finally), Lance and Abby were great together (which gave her hope for her and Chris because if Lance and Abby could do it, then why couldn't she and Chris?), and she was already starting to grow her brand as an artist. Chris was pursuing his dream of playing professional football. Things were falling into place. And she had the love and support of the sweetest guy she'd ever dated and his parents on top of that.

She lifted her face to Chris and he smiled down at her before pressing his lips to hers. It had taken a while to get there, but she was finally getting everything she'd always wanted.

The End

About the Author

Jerica MacMillan is a lifelong reader and lover of romance. Nothing beats escaping into a book and watching people fall in love, overcome obstacles, and find their happily ever after. She was named a semi finalist in Harlequin's So You Think You Can Write 2015 contest.

Jerica is living her happily ever after in North Idaho with her husband and two children. She spends her days building with blocks, admiring preschooler artwork, and writing while her baby naps in the sling. Sign up to join her Book Club at www.JericaMacMillan.com.

Books by Jerica MacMillan

Players of Marycliff University
Summer Fling
Convenient Fall
Managed Hearts
Unsaid Things
Coping Skills
False Assumptions — coming July, 2017!

Rebound Series
Rebound Therapy
Rebound Envy
Rebound Revival